I0750520

Part 1:

I've Gotta Have It

by

**Kimani Lauren**

This is a work of fiction. Similarities to real people, places, or events are entirely coincidental.

HERE I LAY PART 1: I'VE GOTTA HAVE IT

**First edition. June 10, 2021.**



ISBN: 978-1736953938

Written by Kimani Lauren.

To Auntie Janie, who once basically told me to make him drop off the money and leave.

**“Now I know why they say the best things are free...”**

**—Monica**

When I left my hometown, I had dreams of only coming back as a celebrity guest to light the downtown Christmas tree. Being back there, dancing on a tabletop and pouring champagne down my friend's throat wasn't the worst thing I could have been doing for money. It was just the fact that I was supposed to be in Paris getting ready to showcase a clothing line during Fashion Week, and I didn't even understand how I blew it.

Weeks ago, I finally had to deal with the aftermath of letting myself get so depressed that my educational status went from academic probation to expulsion. I shouldn't have let those people at the fashion school I attended tell me I was too fat, too Black, and too ghetto to be a part of their world. I'll own the Black proudly, but my fly suburban ass was far from ghetto. I was from Sapphire Cadre, the place where everyone either owned a house with a white picket fence or was getting ready to move into one. Everyone there was a teacher, bus driver, or worked at the post office for ten or more years. I was the jewel of that town. I'd been all over the world modeling, and I left to get a business degree and go to fashion school so I could launch my own designer label. Ten years later, my label was supposed to be one of the major fashion houses.

Instead, I posed in lingerie for a flyer to entice people to come to a pajama party at The Opal Lounge on the last Saturday night in September. The lace and satin two-piece set I wore to the party clung to my curves and just barely covered what the world didn't need to see for free. All eyes were on me; two sets interested me. First, there was Best. He was the camera man who put me on the flyer. Then, there was this dark and sexy stranger standing at the bar. I'd never seen him before, but I was going to know exactly who he was by the end of the night.

A couple came through the door. That added a third set of eyes on me—a set of eyes that messed up my whole mood. The was they squinted and then enlarged showed disappointment in me being home instead of in ads on the pages of Harper's Bazaar. Foxy Brown and Blackstreet tried to convince me to ignore everything and keep enjoying the way the beat made my hips swing while they sang "Get Me Home," but my friend Brooke just *had* to point out the couple who just walked through the door.

Brooke climbed onto the bar with me and broke my concentration. "Nay-Nay, I know that's not Miguel coming into your spot with another girl!"

While trying to continue rocking to the song, I frowned down at her and barked, "Why would you come up here and make it look like I was paying him any attention?"

She recoiled and asked, "Aren't you mad, though?"

I bucked my eyes at her. "Brooke, do you see what I look like, and do you see what the bitch he's with looks like? He lost, not me."

I couldn't help but glance at my ex while he led his new chick to the dance floor to press against her the way he used to do to me. It was a hell of a way to confirm that I was single.

Miguel had been my boyfriend since I was in the tenth grade. He dealt with fast money and was supposed to be stacking some for me to open a warehouse somewhere in New York City. The night before I left for college, he begged me not to go because he was going to miss me too much. Then, he told me to go and get the degree so that he could send me the money to start my line. That was the last time I heard from him, and that was over a year ago.

After the song ended, I hopped down from the bar and stomped away from Brooke. She tried to follow, but I snapped at her to leave me alone. My friend, Siraya, did come with me and asked if I wanted to leave. I looked over my shoulder and shot a dirty look at Brooke. She was standing there with our other friend, Yolanda, and Siraya's cousin, Yvette, trying to look disinterested in guys who approached her to dance. Everything was irritating all of a sudden. Siraya hooked her arm in mine and led me to the bar.

"You want me to run outside and slash his tires?" she asked me.

"Nope. He's dead to me," I replied, and took a seat.

Rashad, the bartender, came to us immediately. He turned his back to Siraya and leaned between us before he asked me what I wanted.

"I need five of those top-shelf margaritas that you make so good," I told him.

"Aight. I got yours. Whose credit card you putting the other four on?" he inquired.

My face puckered when I answered, "Nobody's. I'm the whole reason why all these people are up in here. My friends all drink for free."

"No. *You* drink for free cuz you a dime," he argued.

"My friends are cute too," I pointed out.

"Your friends are high school cute. You the dime. If they wanna drink, it gotta be on somebody else's dollar," Rashad told me.

I glanced at Siraya, who was too preoccupied to hear the conversation. Instead of paying any more attention to Rashad, I followed her line of sight. The dark stranger was walking toward us with this other fine ass dude. I crossed my legs and told Rashad to go make the drinks.

"Who's paying? Nay, the new manager makes me come out my pocket for anything free I give out that I ain't discussed ahead of time," he complained.

"Chill, Rashad. We got them," the stranger said.

"Oh really? What you supposed to be, some type of baller?" I wondered aloud.

"Ugh. Don't tell me you one of them stuck up chicks," he said.

Before I could think of anything else to say, Rashad clarified, "Banger, she talking about buying five drinks. You got all five?"

"Don't disrespect my pockets like that," the stranger said, and put down money on the bar. "Make sure it's top shelf, too. I know your boss be telling you to charge top shelf for some toilet water."

Rashad cracked up at that and walked away to fill our order.

"Thank you for the drinks," Siraya said.

The stranger's friend made introductions for the two of them. "My name is Rize, and this is Banger." He had some really cute dimples, but he was nothing like his sexy, rugged friend. He was too friendly.

His friend seemed to be disinterested in drawing attention. Neither of them adhered to the pajama dress code. Instead, they opted for sweatpants and white ribbed tank tops. They looked damn good too, but the one named Banger looked slightly better.

"I'm Siraya."

"Pretty name for a beautiful woman," Rize told her. "Your friend got a name, or is she sitting there tryna make one up so that we can't find y'all again after tonight?"

Siraya giggled at that. I gave them my name.

"Monaysia?" Banger repeated, making sure he pronounced it correctly.

I jumped on the defensive and snapped, "Yes. My mother was tired of every baby girl around our way being named either Monique or

Asia, so my parents did something different and combined the two. Monaysia. Go ahead and tell me my name is ghetto, and you don't wanna deal with a chickenhead."

That was only my mother's version of the story. Much later in life, I found out that my father named me after two women he cheated on my mother with. My name was his own personal joke. All that taught me was that men who claimed to love you would embarrass you at any cost. I wasn't about to tell that story in a bar, though. It was bad enough that I was cringing while waiting for his reaction to the story I gave him.

"That's unique. I like it," he said, surprising the hell out of me. He looked around. "Which one of these niggas in here looking at you like they want a problem is your man?" Banger asked.

I felt Miguel's eyes on me but refused to look at him.

"Well, I just found out tonight that I'm single after four years, so none of them." I shrugged and said, "Thank you for the drink."

I slid off the barstool. Siraya and I took the drinks back to the rest of our clique. They were dancing with some cornballs that we knew from high school. I was ready to get out of there, but I still had to judge the pajama contest. A room full of bitches who couldn't even dress better than me in their sleep, and I had to give one of them a prize. I should have been eating baguettes and sketching garments. I gulped down my margarita and went to find my ride.

"Can we do this contest? I'm ready to go?" I asked Best.

His brother, Ronnie, who was also his business partner, frowned and said, "We had hoped you didn't see Miguel in here with Asia."

"Ain't nobody thinking about Miguel. I just have some work to do," I snapped.

"Nay, I can't leave," Best told me. "You know I make the most money after everything shuts down and everybody wants to get those last minute pictures in the parking lot."

I huffed.

"I'll take her home," a woman said from behind them.

I backed up a little. This woman's skin looked like liquid gold. She wore a blonde ponytail that perfectly complimented her skin. Her face and lips were shaped like hearts. I wasn't used to someone in Sapphire Cadre being finer than me.

"I'm their sister, Melinda," she said to me.

"I didn't know you had a sister, Best." I raised an eyebrow.

She giggled and told me, "I'm the problem child they try not to acknowledge. I just stopped in here tonight with some friends and bumped into them. It'll be no problem for me to take you home. I'm pretty bored."

I started to tell her that I would walk home, but then I recognized her as the girl who always came into one of my classes late wearing microscopic skirts and asked, "Aren't you in my Sociology class at SCC?"

The smile she gave me had a warm, sisterly vibe, which made me comfortable enough to ride with her. I asked Best to take the rest of my crew home, but Siraya came with me.

Banger and Rize stood by a Cadillac Escalade when we got to the parking lot. Siraya tried to slap me five behind her back, but I wasn't ready to celebrate quite yet. Just as I suspected, Melinda got into the driver's seat. Coffee cups and empty mascara tubes were all over the place. That pissed me off, because I would never let a car that nice get that dirty. I also wouldn't bother with community college if I could afford a truck like that, but riding in filth was better than being in the same place as my filthy ex and his new bitch.

"Can we take y'all to get something to eat?" Rize offered while Melinda let her truck warm up.

"I can eat a little something-something. How you feeling, Nay?" Siraya asked.

"No, thank you. I need to get home and study," I answered.

"Study for what?" Siraya pushed.

"I have a Sociology exam on Wednesday," I replied.

She squinted at me and jerked her head forward. "Where do you take sociology?"

"Sanford Community College," I replied. "I gotta get my grades up so that I can get out of here."

Siraya shook her head several times before she continued her questioning. "When do you go to SCC?"

"Early mornings and mostly evenings. I go around my work schedule. Before you ask, I work at Sanford Ringer," I snapped.

She shook her head again and blinked. "Friend, how long have you been home?"

I sighed. "Since July or August."

"And this is the first time I'm seeing you?" she exclaimed. "And you're not just here for the weekend?"

I shook my head and said, "Don't tell the rest of those bitches, though. The last thing I need is them laughing at me."

"You know I wouldn't do you like that," she said. "It would have been nice if you told me you were back, though. We could have done dinner after work or something. I work at Sanford Cable. You know that's just next door to your job."

Rize butted in and asked, "So can we take y'all to get something to eat?"

The front passenger door opened before I could answer. A man with a silk bathrobe draped over his forceful physique hopped into the car.

"Let's go hit The Spot. This shit was dead. Leave it to Sapphire Cadre to have a party where the finest chick in the club was the one on the flyer," he said.

Melinda giggled. "That's how it's supposed to be everywhere."

He argued, "Nah. That's supposed to be an advertisement. Like, 'Come here. This girl is gonna be here, and there's gonna be a whole bunch of other girls who look like her.' That shit was like the girl on the flyer, and then every chick in high school who wanted to be down with her and dress like her so she would be their friend."

"Wow!" Siraya exclaimed.

I couldn't help but laugh as he turned around and squinted at us.

"Leave it to y'all to leave with the girl from the damn party poster. What up though, ladies? I'm Trigga."

He turned around. Melinda pulled off.

"I ain't wanna be up in there anyway once I saw that nigga from West Sanford," Rize commented. "So what's up, ladies? Y'all up for a better party, or you just want us to take you to get something to eat and go home?"

"I really gotta get home to study," I said. "Thank you for the offer, but I gotta get my grades up and get outta Sanford County."

Siraya sucked her teeth. "Stop being a model, and put something on your stomach. You got the whole weekend to study. Depending on who you have, I might have an exam from last semester that I can give you to study from."

Melinda turned around in her seat as though there weren't a steering wheel and brakes in front of her. "For real? Girl, I will pay you for whatever notes you have for that class. That lady ain't no joke."

Siraya nodded her head. "So that problem's solved. Come and get something to eat, friend. We're probably too naked to go to another club."

Melinda took that as a signal to get more comfortable with her driving. She jerked that monster of a truck around corners, missed turns, and drove in reverse at one point. I clung to Banger for my life, even though I didn't know him to be trusting him with it. She drove out of our little suburb and to a bridge to get into South Sanford. Siraya and I were always told to stay out of there, but we kept it cool that night. A sheriff standing at the entry made Melinda roll down her window to check her license, but he took one look at that swan neck, seductive eyes, and heart shaped lips and told her to have a good night. She drove forward and gagged.

"What the hell was that? You didn't even do anything," I said.

"Just don't drive down here without your license is all I can say," Melinda warned me.

We went to a 50s style ice cream parlor with black and white checkered floors and red chairs. Rize suggested we get chicken finger subs. I didn't eat too much fried food, but it smelled too good for me to decline.

Instead of sitting in the restaurant, we got back into the car and drove down to the Aliners River, the u-shaped body of water that kept South Sanford separated from the rest of the county. I'd never been that far down the river, but the water sparkled under the moonlight. We sat and had small talk to get to know each other. Banger hadn't said much all night, but Melinda kept the conversation going. Rize asked us if we smoked. When Siraya and I eagerly said that we did, the guys got out of the car. For some reason, Siraya went with them.

"You like working at the phone company?" Melinda asked me.

"Not really. I like getting a paycheck to get me out of here once I get my grades up," I said. "When I put that with the money I make doing flyers for Ronnie and Best, I get closer and closer."

She nodded. Then she took a bite out of her sandwich. After she swallowed it, she said, "You can make a whole lot more at my job. We're having a hiring event tomorrow if you want to come."

I should have asked questions, but she drove an Escalade. I had none that I could think of.

"It's mostly weekends, and you have to go out of town a lot," she continued.

"Who do I make the cover letter out to? I can use as much time away from here as I can get," I grumbled.

She turned around and studied me with sympathy pulling down the corners of her mouth.

"I don't mean to get in your business, but my brother talks about you a lot. A *whole* lot. I mean, I don't speak to my family often, but your name has been coming out of his mouth since he was 12 or 13. He's really happy that you came back home, and all he's been talking about is saving up to send you to Paris next summer since your family emergency brought you back here."

"That's what he told you?" I asked.

"Yup."

I nodded my head. "Then he's a real friend."

"So anyway, I'll pick you up tomorrow and bring you in to meet my boss. We'll be gone all day, so make sure you clear your schedule. And don't worry about having to do this club flyer shit any more either. You're way too gorgeous for that kind of work," she told me.

"Thank you, but I have an arrangement with your brothers. I model for them, and they give me free photoshoots to keep my portfolio updated," I said.

"Oh yeah. Best did say that you were a professional model. Well, I guess that works for you then."

Siraya and the guys came back to the car. Melinda rolled the blunt while Siraya told Rize her whole life story. The way that she was smiling at him and staring into his eyes had me ready to smack her. After what happened to me that night, she should have been done with men the way I was. My attitude went out the window when my fingers touched Banger's as he passed me the spliff. Our eyes linked briefly. Then I looked away and tried not to die choking.

"Damn. I need to cop on this side of the bridge from now on," I said after I recovered. I stared at the river. The sparkle looked like it was turning to bubbles, and it was creeping me out. I couldn't stop looking at it, though. Siraya tapped my knee to get me to pass her the blunt.

"I'm spending the night at your spot, Nay-Nay. Denise and Edwin don't be in your ass about coming home drunk and high the way

Siobhan and Dartanion be in mine," Siraya said when we finished smoking.

Rize asked her, "Do y'all have to go home at all? It's early."

"I gotta be at work at six in the morning. What you doing tomorrow, Nay?"

"I might do an hour or so of OT," I said, staring out the window. "It'll keep me out of Denise and Edwin's house."

"Oh. That's too bad. I had a lot of fun getting to know y'all," Rize said.

Banger hadn't said anything, but he and I kept peeking at each other. I couldn't tell what he was thinking about me. Part of me wanted to tongue him down and strip him naked for the simple fact that he didn't mention those drinks he bought my friends and me after he paid for them. Most of the men I knew would remind me of that for the rest of my life. A bigger part of me just wanted to go home. I was still embarrassed about my ex, and I didn't like it.

We crossed the bridge again. Even though the car smelled like a ganja plantation, Melinda flirted with the sheriff and got us across it quickly.

"We're spending the night at your spot. I ain't going across that shit again," Trigga declared.

Melinda started rattling off what she wanted for breakfast. Her order took the rest of the ride for her to finish. Rize hopped out of the car to walk Siraya to the door. I was surprised when Banger offered to walk with me too. I declined.

"Next time I see you, you better not still have an attitude about a nigga stupid enough to let you go," Banger said.

"And what makes you think you'll ever see me again?" I wondered.

"I'm making sure I bump into you again," he told me. "Good night, Nay-Nay."

I switched my ass through my parents' picket fence and waited for Siraya to give Rize her phone number before we went inside to get fussed at by my parents. It was the first time I came home from a club appearance smelling like I'd been having fun. I was sure my parents would have something to say. They'd had so much to say every day since I'd come back to their house.

It was just my luck that my dad was pulling into the driveway after his normal Friday night of bowling and drinking with his friends. We could smell the Seagram's on him as soon as he opened the door. He stared after the Escalade that we got out of before turning to us.

"Friends of yours?" he asked.

"Yeah. That's a girl from my Sociology class," I replied.

"The one you flunked out of, or the one that you had to come home and retake in community college?" he quipped. He glazed over me sucking my teeth in response and looked to Siraya. "Hey! It's my good daughter who doesn't disappoint me! How's my favorite daughter?"

She giggled. My parents started calling her their favorite when we were in the seventh grade, and they never stopped. It used to be funny. That night, it annoyed me.

The picket fence door swung open once again. I caught a glimpse of a Lexus LX. Three giggling idiots spilled out of it. Brooke and Yvette dragged Yolanda. I glared at them through narrowed eyes.

"She's too drunk to take home. We gotta stay here tonight," Yvette announced.

Even though the gate was closed, I was stuck staring as though I could still see the LX.

"I wish you'd stayed in The City, Nay. We were supposed to be spending weekends with you and doing all kinds of fly stuff. What happened?" Brooke asked in a baby voice that told me she really didn't care.

"When you find out how she blew three scholarships, let me know," Dad said, and stomped into the house.

I whispered to them, "Was that Miguel's car you just got out of?"

"Girl, he had to give us a ride home. Ronnie and Best were too busy hiding under the bar with Rashad," Brooke answered.

"Hiding under the bar for what?" Siraya wanted to know.

"Somebody started fighting and shooting," Yvette answered. "I knew it was gonna get bad when the South and the West were in there at the same time. Why'd you leave?"

"I have to study, and I have to be at work at six in the morning," I answered. "Was the girl Miguel was with mad that you had to ride with him?"

"She was the one who got shot!" Yvette declared. "This was the craziest night we've had in a long time, Nay-Nay. You being home really makes all the difference."

My eyes bucked. "He left her there?"

Yvette shrugged. "Nothing he could do about it. He jumped away from her and toward us, got scared when he saw you weren't with us, and made us get in his car, thinking you would come with us. Then, he got mad and brought us here."

"Why here?" I wondered.

"Why are we talking about him? Who were those two cuties you left with?" Yvette demanded to know. "Do they have more friends who look like them? I saw the darker one looking at me while you were wasting champagne, Monaysia."

Everyone cut their eyes at her, but no one commented.

"I have no idea who those people were. I just knew the girl from my sociology class. She was leaving, and I was ready to go." I snorted out a laugh. "I can't believe Best hopped under the bar and left y'all."

Siraya scrunched her face and perked her ears. "Is somebody throwing rocks at your window?"

Brooke and Yvette left Yolanda laying in the grass and struggled to dash behind Siraya and me. We went around the back and saw Best throwing rocks at my window the way he used to back when we were in high school and sneaking out of my room to sneak into that same club we'd just been in. Siraya and I cracked up. Yvette and Brooke were not amused. They cussed him out before he got to them. He ignored them and gave me a dirty look.

"What's your problem? Why would you leave my friends?" I snapped.

"I thought you were so sad that you only wanted to stay low key?" he snapped back.

"Why do you think I left?" I asked. "And why did you leave my friends?"

"Ask Brooke," Best said.

"Ask me what? Ask why I tried to jump back there with you, and you blocked me!" she yelled.

They started arguing. I rested a little. Things were back to the way I knew them. I left them right out there while Yvette went back to the front lawn and struggled to get Yolanda off the ground. She asked if we were going to help. Siraya and I snickered at her and sat on my front stairs. We split the rest of the chicken finger sub I had left over from that car ride and didn't offer Yvette any.

"Okay, friend. We gotta close our eyes for a couple of hours," Siraya reminded me when we were done eating.

"What are you gonna do about all these people on your lawn?" Yvette wondered.

I'd forgotten about Brooke and Best bickering just that quick. I yelled for Best to get Yolanda home and started going inside with Siraya. Yvette scurried behind us. We looked at her quizzically.

"If Siraya's staying here, I know it's because you're giving her a ride to work tomorrow. I need a ride too," she told us.

We huffed and went inside.

My dad sat in the living room with my mother. They must have been talking about me, because both of their faces were twisted when they looked at us.

"Hi, good daughter. Hi, Yvette," my mother greeted them. "I see Monaysia made you some free outfits. Funny how she can do that for you all but couldn't do it in school, where it counted."

I started to argue with my mother about what she said, but I was tired of arguing with her. We argued every minute up until Best pulled in front of my house and beeped his horn earlier that evening. She'd voiced her issues with me being there. Going back and forth again was useless.

My mother was a part of a super self-important group of women who met for dinner every Friday night to brag about what their daughters were doing over cheddar bay biscuits and Lobsteritas. Up until summer's end, Mommy won the non-existent prize. She had two daughters going to college; one at Syracuse University studying to be a mathematician, the other getting a dual degree at NYU and a reputable fashion school so that she and her clothing designs could grace the pages of *Vogue* and *Harper's Bazaar*. When I came back, she couldn't tell those same tales. She had nothing to worry about. I was out of there soon.

Siraya, Yvette, and I continued toward the stairs. My father called my name and stopped me.

"Your mother and I discussed and agreed that we want you to start paying bills. You need to provide your four most recent pay stubs so that we can figure out something reasonable and work our way up to you paying one-third of the household expenses."

My mouth dropped open while Yvette snickered. I hoped that hiring event with Melinda amounted to something. Getting back to Paris would have to wait. I was getting out of Denise and Edwin's house first.

"Dropped out of school just to come back here and model for free," Daddy mumbled. "I can't believe that *my* daughter went from a real runway to a rapper hoochie."

Mommy's eyes bucked. "Edwin, stop letting your liquor speak for you."

"Why? She came back here, crying and not talking for weeks. If she has the will to get up suddenly, then she can pay some bills. She's not wasting her time here making things for a bunch of drunks laying out on the lawn. And she's not bringing that underaged alcoholic over here any more either. She's just as embarrassing as her father," Dad ranted.

Mommy tilted her head and asked, "How much money did you lose to him tonight?"

Dad turned to her with shame stretching his eyes and mouth into discs. "It's not as bad as you think."

"If you're telling your daughter to pay a third of the bills when you're already making her pay for community college, then it's worse than I think. How much did you lose?" Mommy demanded.

"Denise..."

"Edwin!"

I yanked Yvette up the stairs and shoved her into my sister Kidra's room while Siraya came into mine. When Yvette went back and told her parents what my parents were arguing about, there was going to be a huge mess. They would all make up from it the next time one of us went back to our parents with mess from someone else's house, but I didn't plan to be in the mix long enough to give my parents their time in the sun.

Siraya put on her pajamas, climbed into my bed, and stared at me.

"We about to have pillow talk?" I asked, and forced a giggle.

She fluffed my pillow dramatically and patted it. "Come lay in my arms, honey, and tell mama what's wrong."

I giggled at her. "Leave me alone."

Her tone switched to a serious one. "Nay-Nay, what happened for real? Because I know you didn't let being heartbroken over Miguel push you back home."

"No, and lower your voice. I don't want Yvette making up any shit like that and spreading it around Sapphire Cadre," I told her.

Siraya sucked her teeth. "I don't know why you don't think that she didn't tell the whole world you came back here and sat on Miguel's doorstep and cried during that one Christmas break, but she did. I cleaned it up and told them you heard he got caught up in a drug bust and couldn't find out which jail he was in. With all the drug busts they've had in West Sanford since you've been gone, it was easy to make everyone believe."

That was Siraya, my unpaid PR agent. I loved that girl so much for always clearing up my name and keeping me in a positive light.

"Thank you, friend," I said.

Her eyes saddened. "Tell me what happened for real, friend."

I sighed and tried not to cry while I went into the story of my year in fashion school. I had the choice between going to FIT and a slightly lesser known school. Dororthy Aldrige, who was the head of the modeling agency I started with, took scholarship offers from the lesser known school directly to my parents. I wanted to go to FIT, but the New York College of Design, Textiles and Fashion gave a full ride. To sweeten the pot, Mrs. Aldridge introduced them to a dual degree program with NYU. My desires to go to FIT were never listened to again.

At first, my school experience wasn't bad. I was floating off of living my dream. Everything was such a rush. I was always running from one campus to the next, getting the train, going to calls. I was so busy that I missed coming home for my first Thanksgiving. One of my classes was asked to ride a float in the parade. I was on national TV.

Then, things started changing once I got home for Christmas. It didn't hit me until then that Miguel hadn't answered any of my calls or written me back the few times I found to write to him. I called him when my body adjusted to being able to relax. He didn't answer, and I was only home for a few days, so I piled my girls into my dad's car, drove into West Sanford, and looked every place I knew he might be. I never felt more stupid in my whole life.

That put me in a bad mood when I got back to school. Maybe I was sensitive, but the designers I sat with told me I was gaining weight. That was a lie, but I added an extra hour of lifting and cardio to my morning workouts. I rarely had time to eat. I was afraid of losing my curves, but I was looking better than ever. My frame belonged in a picture on teenage boys' walls. There were a lot of complaints about the size of my knockers fitting into the bras they wanted me to wear, but that was stupid. What sold a bra better than a nice pair of knockers?

No matter how good I looked, it got exhausting to hear how fat I was every day. After the fat comments sank in, my design professors lumped on the critique that I needed to let go of the ghetto. That comment used to piss me off the most. I didn't know anything about brick apartment buildings where people peed on the elevator floor. I only heard about them when Miguel talked crap about the Cesar Chavez and Nat Turner Projects. There was nothing ghetto about me, but they told me my designs needed to start reflecting that.

Once they saw that critique got to me, they hurled a different insult at me every day. Most of my classmates told me that I was imagining the critiques. Others told me I was being too sensitive, but I was the only Black girl who lasted more than a semester there. After I survived my first year, they turned up the pressure to push me out.

The thing that pushed me over the edge was the night I was supposed to leave for Paris Fashion Week. I had my best sketches wrapped carefully and had just shipped my entire collection. There was a letter delivered to me that my grades had slipped below the required GPA, but I'd decided months before that I couldn't care about that. Fashion school was taking up all of my studying time. I'd passed the business and marketing classes that I was interested in already. NYU could wait for me to come back from Paris before I got my stuff together in undergrad. My main focus was getting on that plane and showing my collection.

I pulled my luggage into our agreed upon destination. The students selected looked at me as though I had an elbow growing out of my forehead. I was used to that, so I ignored them and pulled my luggage along with me to check in. My toughest teacher and critic, Matteo Fabiola, glared at me. He demanded to know why I thought I was getting on the plane with them. I showed him the letter that he wrote me showing that I'd been accepted into Paris Fashion Week. He peered at it.

"Oh. You were chosen as an alternate. I neglected to inform you that you're not needed."

My heart sank. My whole line was already in Paris, but I wasn't going to be there. How was that possible? I went back to my dorm and waited for my clothes, patterns, and sketches to be returned to me. Even after I got kicked out of school, I took the last of the money I had and stayed in a hotel while I waited for the class to return with my possessions. Matteo Fabiola never returned, and neither did my designs. I spoke to the heads of the school, but they said there was nothing I could do about it. They basically blamed me for sending my stuff to Paris ahead of me. That was what made me come back home.

"So when are you getting your work back?" Siraya asked when I finished pouring my heart out.

"Probably never," I answered.

"Friend! That sounds worse than the music business!" Siraya exclaimed with sadness in her voice.

"We probably run into the same stupid scammers," I said. "It's been so hard being back here."

"I know it has." She cooed. "Outside of track and field season, I can't remember a whole month when you've stayed here. Do you like your job, at least?"

I scoffed. "What's there to like? I listen to people complain about their bills all day. All I know is that I'm never paying bills if owing people money for things that you use makes you yell at strangers at 9 in the morning. Who does that?"

Siraya frowned and sighed. "You're supposed to have better than this. You've been working since you were seven."

"It's not all bad," I told her. "I'm trying to get into the marketing and advertising department there. My commercials and ads could be the bomb if they let me in. That's why I'm going to work early in the morning. I'm gonna stand outside of Channel 3 and slip my look book to Hope Thomas. Maybe I can get on as her wardrobe stylist, and then I'm gonna post up outside of the director of marketing's office and sell myself to her."

Dropping Yvette off at her job the next morning made me too late to do anything more than flirt with a security guard and listen to him lie to me about getting my book to the morning anchor woman. I knew he was going to put it in the trash as soon as I got back into my car, but I was determined to keep trying. After dropping Siraya off, I went to the fourth floor at my job with my resume in my hand.

The people who worked on that floor had the luxury of not working during the weekends, so I was surprised to see there was someone working just a few cubicles down from the director's office. He raised a coffee cup in my direction as a polite greeting. I barely mumbled something back while I posted myself outside of the glass doors to Amy Ruffin's office with my resume and cover letter. She came to her office every Saturday morning for exactly one hour. Most times, she was with the c-suite and president of the company. Even though Saturdays were supposed to be casual, I made sure that I was wearing a suit and pearls to make me stand out. Just before the elevator chimed to announce it was letting off passengers, I twisted my hair into a bun on top of my head.

"Good morning, Amy," I said to the yellow woman wearing a Sanford Ringer t-shirt, jeans, and loafers. "My name is Monaysia Giles—"

She assessed me from head to toe and exclaimed, "What a suit! Did Jackson's Department Store get a new line in without calling me?"

I tugged at my suit jacket and tried to hide my grin. "No. This is something that I made myself."

Her eyes widened. "Really? Wow!" Then, she frowned and asked, "Why are you making your own clothes? Are you poor? You must work in customer service."

It took everything out of me not to cuss her out, but I tugged at my jacket again and shuffled my feet while I took a deep breath. "No, I'm not poor. I'm an aspiring fashion designer. I modeled for Naomi Iman for many years and fell in love with fashion. And, yes, I do work in customer service, but I'm coming to you because I'd be of better use to you than them. I'm here from NYU, and I specialize in marketing. Here's my resume. I'm confident you'll see I speak your language and would be an amazing translator of that in print as well as in television advertisements."

I put the cover letter and resume in her hands and waited for her to speak.

"Naomi Iman, you say? I'm great friends with the leader of that organization, Dorothy Aldridge. I'll ask about you." She turned to walk away.

Rushing behind her, I countered, "Why ask her when I'm right here? I'd love to further discuss what value I bring."

She spun around and gave me a glare that told me not to move a step further.

"Do you know why I come here every Saturday morning?" Before I could guess, she continued, "It's to get away from my family. My work for the week is done on Thursday, unless one of our competitors drops some huge bomb. I have three children and a husband, and all they do is talk all day. Do you really think that I want to talk to you?"

"It probably wasn't written on your Rolodex, but you'll find value in our conversation. I'm here to get away from my family as well. Finding me a position in your department would be a win for both of us, but a bigger win for you. Enjoy your Saturday and your quiet."

I turned around and nearly bumped into the CEO of the company, Fetu Po. He was so short I had to look down to apologize.

He looked up at me. "My apologies," he said with every tooth in his mouth showing.

"No, Mr. Po. That was all my fault. I was just down here letting Mrs. Ruffin know what value I can add to your marketing department as someone here from NYU." I reached into my satchel and handed him a copy of my resume and cover letter. "Perhaps the two of you can take a look at my credentials and let me know what you think on your next business day. I do understand the value of a quiet Saturday. Enjoy yours."

Confidently I strutted away from them and sat through two torturous hours of work. Hopefully, this hiring event at Melinda's job would get me out of there.

After work, I picked up Yvette and Siraya. Yvette whined that she wanted me to treat her to lunch, so I dropped her off at 147th Street and told her to walk a few blocks over to compete with the hookers. She was steaming as she ran after my car. I stopped and let her back in, laughing at the deep shade of red her anger made her. Siraya and I cracked up the whole way home. Yvette got out and slammed the car door.

"So what's up with those guys we met last night? Are we going out with them tonight or what?" Siraya asked after Yvette was out of sight.

"We met guys last night?" I asked. I'd kind of forgotten about everything that didn't have anything to do with money.

"Yes. They wanted to take us out tonight, but I gotta figure something out. Me and Yolanda are supposed to be meeting these record execs," she said.

"Concentrate on the money, not the men," I instructed.

"You're right, friend. Thanks for the ride. Call me!"

I waited until her picket fence was closed before I continued to my house.

Before I got both feet through the door, my mother fussed at me about the four paycheck stubs she asked me for.

"I haven't even worked there long enough to get four paycheck stubs," I reminded her.

"Well, you need to start writing down every single thing you buy for the next four weeks. If you're going to be spending money on yourself, then you're going to be giving us money first," Mommy said.

With my hands on my hips, I said, "Denise Giles, do you see what I look like? Most of this came from you. Why would anyone who walked out the house looking like us have to pay for anything anywhere at any time?"

She smiled at me, the green in her eyes piercing holes through mine. "You're absolutely right. I knew you being here would be good for something." She took the keys from me and strutted out the house.

My pager went off. I checked my voicemail and heard Melinda telling me she was on her way to get me. While I waited for her, I pulled the bun to the back of my head and read over my resume. That was the first time it dawned on me that I had no idea what the position I was going for entailed. That wasn't a big deal. I could sell anything.

That black, shiny Escalade pulled in front of my house, and I couldn't help but think it was my carriage out of Hell. I checked my satchel to count how many copies of my resume I was taking with me. There were only ten. I asked Melinda if she minded taking me back to my job to print some more, but she just giggled a little and told me that ten copies were more than enough.

"Just be you. This job is more based on personality. They want to see how you carry yourself and how you carry a conversation. That's the biggest part of this job: talking about you and your value," Melinda said. "I'm almost sure you'll get hired on the spot. Don't quit your day job yet, though. This is good money, but it doesn't come with health insurance yet."

I sighed. I was looking forward to not hearing people scream into my ear about how high their phone bills were anymore.

"That suit is really nice. Best told me that you started making most of your clothes in the tenth grade. Did you make that?"

"Thank you. Yes." I answered while reading over my resume.

She snatched it from me. "Girl, if you don't relax! Look. Don't go in here desperate, because you'll be handling clients who will be able to smell it on you and trying to low ball you when it comes time to talk about pay."

I put my resume into my satchel and closed it. We rode across that bridge again. The sheriff flirted with both of us before letting us cross.

"What's the point of that?" I asked.

"If they don't like the way you look, they pull you out your car and search it for drugs and hostages," she answered.

I laughed at that, but she didn't. Instead, she whipped her SUV around potholes until we got to a plaza. The savory scent of soul food from a restaurant next door called Peter's Kitchen slightly overpowered the sweet smell of oil sheen and the smell of fresh cut lumber coming from a store called Furniture Revolution. When a door opened a few doors down at a shop called Kenyan Bean, coffee joined the air. It almost could have been a perfume. We went to a dark wooden part of the plaza. The words "Hair Revolution" were on a sign above it.

"Everything is on me today, so don't look at prices, and keep your bag closed," she told me as we went inside.

The shop was upscale. The doors were made from cherry wood. All the beauty shops I went to before had that glass door where you could see right into the shop, but this one wanted to keep the customers private. It felt like you needed a VIP pass to get in, and that's just what Melinda had.

She took me past the peasant customers and led me upstairs to a room where girls who looked like they were auditioning for a Luke video sat. She introduced me to an array of women in assorted shades of brown. The lead beautician's name was Lynn, and I could tell by the way her lip curled when she looked at me that she didn't like me.

Anyway, the top heavy woman with the deep dimples and generous set of hips, thighs, ass, and stomach told me to come sit in her chair. Her eyes outlined my frame the whole time I walked toward her. I didn't have a problem telling her I didn't get down like that. She told me I wasn't cute enough to be turning anyone down, even though she wasn't trying to get with me.

"Okay, but why are you staring at me like that if you don't want me?" I had to ask, since her eyes kept landing on my best parts.

"Melinda said we might be able to use you on the team. The walk is okay, but with that voice and attitude, I'm not sure. Come sit down and let me doll you up. Then I'll be able to make a decision." Lynn patted her chair.

So this was a modeling job? Well, I was the professional, so this hiring event needed to be going a little differently.

"My walk got me to the runways in New York City, Tokyo, and Paris. I saw my face on the boxes of perm in that case by the door when I walked in. You should be happy I'm here."

Lynn glared at me. I closed my mouth. I sat down in her chair to see what she was talking about. When I looked around at the dozen or so women, it was obvious that somebody had top notch skills. I'd never have to hear about being too Black for them to find a makeup artist for me or to properly light my photos. Lynn took down my weave and started roasting it.

"Girl, you still using hair out of the pack and got the nerve to think somebody wants your low budget ass? And you bragging about a perm box like it's a magazine cover! Girl, I sell that. I don't use that shit in here!" She roared.

Everyone laughed at my weave. Some of the employees thudded up the stairs to see what had them laughing so hard. Melinda giggled as she went through a rack of clothing. I didn't normally let people pick out my clothes, but I was surrounded by high end garments.

When I looked in the mirror, my reflection shocked me. I didn't think it was possible for me to get any prettier, but my eyes were brighter, and the make up pimped out the green in them. My skin looked richer and smoother than ever. The sew-in looked like my hair grew a foot longer and much thicker. I couldn't stop swinging and fluffing it. I looked like sex from my head to my neck.

When we were back in her car, Melinda told me, "I kind of lied to you. When I said this was a hiring event, I really meant I'm going on a date, and I need you to talk to his friend. You don't have to do anything but talk to him, and he'll pay you thousands of dollars. Just come and see if you like it. If you don't, I won't bother you again."

Melinda just didn't know that she'd said the magic words. Dates for dollars was the only way I rolled outside of Miguel. Even Miguel knew to bring me gifts whenever he came to take me anywhere. That was way better than a hiring event. I'd kissed enough ass for one day.

I was feeling pretty damn sexy as I stepped out of the shop wearing a designer who turned me down for a show. Melinda led me through the back lot to two black SUVs with the words "Geno's Auto Sales" painted in script on the sides and on the plates. Beside them stood about five fine ass men and one ugly one. All eyes were on me. The ugly one came up to me first. I hoped Melinda didn't think that was a joke.

"Damn. You look like a caramel sundae. Can I get a lick?"

I couldn't figure out why he was so vocal. My eyes went past him and zeroed in on Banger. He fell back a little when I looked his way. Since he played shy, I glanced at the chubby one standing next to him because he was cute too, and fat guys loved to spend money and eat pussy.

Melinda put her arm out to keep the ugly one away from me.

"We're riding with Banger and Shondell. You know your baby mama be trippin when you get around new girls, and I don't wanna have to whoop her ass today," Melinda barked.

I was a lot more excited to be around Banger than the night I met him. He was so damn tall, and he looked mean as hell. I had something in between my legs I wanted him to be mean to. We got in the second row of an MPV with him and the cute chubby one. Shondell drove, and Banger sat in the back seat without saying a word. I kept catching glimpses of him looking at me through the rearview mirror. He was so damn fine that I wanted him to lean forward and start kissing me on the back of my neck.

We rode to a mansion in Albany. Shondell got out of the car and walked to some white man who looked like he just came from playing golf. I was shook. Melinda didn't seem like the type to date white men. This was a waste of her time. White men thought I was too fat, loud, black, and ghetto. Shondell got back in the car and pulled the car around the back.

"I'm gonna hook you up with David. All you gotta do is talk to him. He won't ask you for no sex," Melinda said as though she was doing me a favor.

I was shaking the whole time, wondering how I'd be rejected. I followed her to a room where David was laying in a bed. He was a tiny, shriveled up little man whose smile grew when he saw me. What kind of date was this?

He took a bottle of pills out of his pocket. "Looks like I got to the doctor just in time to get that prescription of Viagra."

I didn't know that I could run so fast in heels, but I took it back to my high school track days and broke out of that mansion. I got right back in that van and was met with Banger's gun.

"You aight?" he asked, lowering it when he recognized me.

"Hell no! Do you know what they're doing up there?" I hissed.

He looked at me through squinted eyes. "Why'd you come if you didn't want to do it?"

I looked at him like he'd lost his mind. "I didn't know I was coming to do this. Where is a pay phone? I need a cab so I can get out of dodge."

"Nah, just sit here. We'll get you home when they get done."

Melinda came back to the vehicle, laughing at me. "I'm sorry. Ronnie and Best made it seem like you'd be down. My fault. I should've known better than to listen to them."

I perked up like a dog getting ready to attack. "What you mean they made it seem like I was down. All that I've ever done was take pictures for them. How did we get down to fuck old white men from that?"

She waved her hand like she was trying to erase what she just said. "I shouldn't have said that. They just always talked about how good you looked, and I agreed when I saw you. I mean, *I* just made 15 Gs doing this. I thought someone who had to pay for school on her own could use that kind of cash."

"Of course I could use that kind of money, but this ain't the type of shit you just spring on somebody. You said go on a date. I had something totally different in mind."

"Could you get the fuck out the car talking about this shit?"

That mean voice turned me on. I hadn't had any since Best picked me up from the train station in August. I needed something better than what he gave. Banger rarely smiled and rarely had anything to say, which meant he rarely said anything stupid. It made me so wet.

Anyway, Melinda took me back inside the mansion and left Banger to do whatever it was he was supposed to do. She and I went into the kitchen and sat at the table, drinking white wine and talking. I offered to take back the clothes I had on, but she said I could keep them as an apology for the misunderstanding. She also told me that David usually just started talking and fell asleep. When he woke up, he'd swore he'd done something and then paid her an obscene amount of money.

As soon as she said that, a girl named Peaches came downstairs and announced that David was asleep.

"You wanna make some easy money? Now is your opportunity," Melinda offered.

Peaches took me by the hand and coached me on how to slip into the bed with him. Since she was the one who got him to fall asleep, she slipped in on the other side. His hand gripping my knockers didn't feel creepy like I thought it would. I just imagined it was Banger. Although, something in Banger's voice told me he wouldn't fall asleep before he got a chance to hit.

When David woke up, he cried out, "Oh!" and had the craziest look on his wrinkled face.

"I took care of two of you, huh? Well, I can't take these pills anymore. My heart won't be able to take it!"

Just like that, he gave each of us thousands of dollars in cash. Later, I found out that was some New York State tax dollars that I had in my possession. It made me consider becoming Melinda's protégée.

Peaches fingered the clip David took the money out of and then dragged her finger down his leg.

"Is that a Mont Blanc?"

He grinned. "I knew my favorite designer girl would take notice and love this."

"I do love when you introduce me to luxury, David," she said.

I sucked my teeth and rolled my eyes at it. "A Dunhill would have been a better choice for a man like you."

Peaches cut her eyes at me but then looked down at the clip. "You're right. Dunhill is for a more prestigious man. Mont Blanc is for a classic look."

David smiled at us. "Two fashion girls. You design clothes like Peaches does too?"

"I just graduated from FIT, actually," I lied.

"I've been trying to send Peaches there for years. Maybe you can talk her into letting me."

He fell asleep again, and Peaches and I discussed fabrics and some job she was getting in Italy. After David woke up and paid us the second time, we both kissed his cheeks and then went out to the car to discuss silks and Saks Fifth Avenue's corporate job availability.

The ride back was supposed to be in silence, per Banger's decree, but I didn't do quiet car rides. Who can sit in the car for hours without singing along with the radio? Plus, I couldn't stop laughing about the way David woke up. And for once in Sanford County, someone besides the competitive birds at Naomi Iman knew something about some damn quality fashion. Everybody else was on Fubu and the hip-hop brands, but Peaches knew all about the major fashion houses. Banger could just beat my ass if he didn't like life in his car rides.

From the front seat, the other girl who was with us, Cream, kept holding back laughs when I brought up David and telling us to be quiet. I thought I caught Banger almost smiling at me through the mirror's reflection, but it could have just been my imagination.

"Well, sorry we won't get to hang out much more on the weekends," Melinda said as she pulled in front of my house. "But let me know if you change your mind. I hope you had fun this weekend."

"I did. Thanks," I told her. "I'm doing a party for your brothers next week if you want to come."

"We'll see, girl." She touched up her lipstick in the mirror. "If I don't get a job, then I'll come through to see you. If not, we can just do dinner or something after class."

It was about eleven when I walked into the house that night. My parents were sitting on the couch, about to grill me about where I was, but they looked at the skirt suit that I wore and figured I did some overtime at the phone company. I didn't know what their problem was anyway. Me being out the house meant they didn't have time to be mad at me for sitting around their house.

After I got done studying the next night, the phone in my room rang. Even though I hated paying bills, I gladly gave up the money for my own line, because my parents would bug out if their phone rang after nine. I almost didn't hear it since the ringer was so low, but I caught it just at the tenth ring.

"Girl... Banger asked about you," Melinda sang into the phone. "He wants to know if you can come out."

I sat up in bed instantly and thought about the mean boy sitting in the back row of that van with all that hair standing wildly atop his head. The quiet ones always had hammers, and I was badly in need of a pounding. I agreed to go back out. Even though it was almost October, it was warm, so I put on some shiny lime green shorts that presented my hips and thighs as a nice package. My objective for that night was to show him skin so that he'd want to fuck me. Then he could start spending money on upgrading my wardrobe.

"Where are you going now?" Daddy pressed me. "Don't you have school and work tomorrow?"

"Please, Daddy. I was partying way harder than this at school in The city and still made it to class every day," I said.

"And yet you're back here. Maybe it's time to change some of your habits so that you can get back in the game. You're too beautiful to live and die in Sanford County, Monaysia," Daddy said to me.

I put my hands over my heart. "That's the nicest thing you've said to me since I came back."

Daddy frowned at me. I stopped at the mirror on the wall by the front door to make sure my hair still looked good. I didn't know how that lady got those bundles to lay so right, but I never wanted anyone else to do my hair but her.

"That's a pretty expensive looking hairdo," my mother said, watching me fluff and swing it in the mirror. "Seems like if you can afford a weave like that, then you can contribute your third of the bills right now."

I froze and then connected my eyes to hers. "Mommy, please don't joke like that."

Mommy put her hand on her hip. "Now what makes you think it's a joke? You squandered all of our hard earned money in college—"

I turned to her and threw my hands in the air. "I did not squander anything! All you had to do was buy me stuff for my dorm, and Naomi Iman gave me most of that. You haven't paid for much of anything for me since I graduated from high school!"

"And we weren't supposed to have to after you started modeling professionally!" my mother shot back. "You are supposed to be in Paris or Milan right now. That Isiac girl who did Naomi Iman with you hasn't even graduated yet, but she's out there. Why aren't you with her? You're much cuter than she is."

"Dang, Mommy! How many times do I have to tell you that those white people said I was too fat to be in fashion?"

"You should have fought that. Once upon a time, Naomi Campbell was too Black to be in fashion, but she opened a door for you. You should have opened a door for someone else."

That was my mother's favorite wack ass argument.

"Mommy, I am sorry that you were ugly in high school or whatever this is about, and want to use me for revenge, but I can't do it for you. Ask Kidra." I looked in the mirror and panicked. I'd already washed off my makeup. What if Banger didn't like me fresh faced? I reached into my bag and pulled out lipstick and a liner.

"Your sister is already in a good school, getting ready to be an accountant. When will you ever do something like that with your life?" Daddy asked me.

It hurt every time he said that, but I wasn't about to let him know that. "Let me get old enough to drink first, and then I'll do just like you and get a job that makes me spend my Friday nights at the bars." I winked at him and heard a horn honk.

"Monaysia, where are you going? We still have to discuss these bills."

More than anything, I wanted to just hand her a stack of money and tell her to keep the change, but I didn't need her questioning where I got that kind of cash. So I told her I'd write her a check out of my financial aid refund for school in the morning and sashayed out the house.

The same MPV that we rode in earlier sat at the curb in front of my house. This time, Banger was driving. Melinda sat in the back with the dude named Trigga. She clung to him as though he were her teddy bear. They swore they were just best friends, but those two held each other like they were in love.

Banger's eyes went to my thighs in the lime green shorts I wore and stayed there awhile.

"What up?" He greeted me and asked what I wanted to do.

My neck started rolling when I told him, "You called my girl and asked about me, so you tell me what you planned to do when you got me."

"Tell him, girl. Don't let these niggas waste your time," Melinda cheered me on from the back. Trigga told her to shut up. They both laughed.

Banger didn't like holding conversations inside of buildings, whatever that meant, so he took me to the patio of a restaurant in South Sanford called The Midnight Rose Garden. The way people my parents' ages talked about men from that side of the bridge, I didn't expect to be taken somewhere like that. They called their houses dilapidated and said their children weren't worth shit. Looking at Banger and Trigga led me to believe a bunch of old bitches just got turned out and left behind and turned bitter about it.

I saw something way different than what those people were talking about from the minute Banger told me to get whatever I wanted off the menu. At first I rolled my eyes, thinking we were at some diner, but that menu had crab cakes and liquor infused ice cream. He told me they carried the best Chablis in the county. My parents and their friends made it sound like boys from South Ridge couldn't even spell Chablis.

Two more people joined us, Rize and some other girl who looked oddly like Siraya. With Rize, I learned it was best to not even learn the names of the girls he brought around, because he'd have a new one before you knew it. They all fit the same description: 5'5" - 5'7", big eyes, skinny, more legs than torso, boobs not aggressive enough to be called knockers, and bubble butts. He and Trigga spoke to each other more than they did their dates, but Banger was really into me. It was a total turnaround from the brooding boy sitting in the third row during our trip earlier.

He asked me all types of questions that made it seem like he really wanted to get to know me. I showed him the little book of modeling pictures I carried around with me, and he told me he would love to see me in commercials and whatever else he could see me in. I thought he'd get bored listening to me talking my model life, but he kept encouraging me to keep the conversation going.

"I'm not as hot in New York City as I am here," I admitted. "Here I'm considered, like, a premium girl, but I'm just average in New York."

"That's some hater shit. Ain't shit average about you as far as my eyes can tell," he said to me.

I blushed and giggled.

Finally, he asked me if I talked to anyone else, and I had to stumble over that question. My relationship with Melinda's brother blurred some lines, but it wasn't anything serious enough to mention. He obviously didn't say anything to his sister about it. Why would she have me on this date with another dude if he did? Still, I figured it wouldn't hurt to be up front.

"I know you saw my situation at the club last night, but I'm rarely ever single," I told him.

"Well, cut off whatever you got going on," he commanded.

I flipped my hair. "Make it worth my while, and I just might think about it."

By the time our food came, he and I had talked about a million things. He thought I was crazy for paying for school on my own with the way my parents were treating me, but he said he really respected my hustle. He lived with his grandmother so that he could pay all of her bills. I thought that was cute and wondered how I could be down. Grandmothers couldn't live forever, and he'd probably need someone else's bills to pay after she was gone. He was twenty and had one younger brother. He told me not to ask him about his parents, and I respected his wishes. Our conversation kept a smile on my face all night.

Another couple joined us when we were halfway finished with dinner. The girl's name was Shanae, and she looked like a Cabbage Patch in the face but had a body that belonged in a Master P video. Her ugly boyfriend's name was Squeak. I remembered him as the one who called me a caramel sundae before we took our trip. Shanae was pregnant, though, so I was confused by the audacity. She had a subwoofer for a voice box, and he spoke to her like she was garbage. I got irritated by their arguments and wanted to get away from them.

Instead of buying her a meal, he told her to wait to see if any of us had any leftovers that we'd be willing to share with her. A stomach turning episode of secondhand embarrassment came from that, so I bought her something to eat. I was a dumb ass, because everybody was smart enough to teach her ass through tough love. If she sat there and let his ugly ass treat her like that, then she deserved to be treated like that.

Rize took Trigga and Melinda home so that Banger and I could spend more time together. He warned me to never do anything nice for the pregnant girl again, because she was a moocher who needed to leave Squeak alone. He told me they had more kids at home, and he had yet to do right by any of them. I didn't care. What they did on their own time wasn't my business. I just wasn't going to eat in front of a pregnant woman without feeding her. Whatever.

He drove for a little bit and then parked by the Aliners River. The river's water seemed to sparkle in that particular section. I thought he wanted to talk some more, but he leaned over and kissed me instead. You ever had a kiss that made you feel it in the tips of your toes? You ever had somebody make your head spin just by pressing his lips against yours? That's what my first kiss with Banger was like. I didn't want to take my mouth off his, but he kissed me on every part of my body that wasn't covered by clothing. I was open.

The craziest part of that night was that he just stopped. He put his arm around me, laid my head on his chest, and let me fall asleep. I thought maybe he felt a way about me whoring myself out earlier, but Banger didn't care about that. Maybe he didn't have any rubbers, but I was soaking wet. I knew he could feel it through the sateen and spandex blend of my shorts. Confused, I fell asleep.

"What you gotta do today?" he asked me when I woke up. The sun was up. The clock on the dash said it was a little after six.

"School, work, back to school," I told him as I stretched. "Then I got a little photoshoot to do."

He offered to drop me off at school but told me he had a stop to make first. We rode down to the Nat Turner Projects. I'd been down there a time or two for the summer basketball tournaments, but I'd never had any reason to go inside of those buildings. I was always told the projects smelled like pee, but they just smelled like food and a million different body sprays and air fresheners.

A group of boys stood on the stoop in front of a high-rise. The railings were painted a horrendous shade of green. All of the boys gawked at me, but they only spoke to Banger. They made sure to speak up so that he acknowledged each of them. He addressed them all by names I'd only halfway commit to memory but didn't introduce me to them. We went up fourteen ugly green staircases to an apartment on the top floor. Children were all over the place.

"Are all of these your kids?"

My voice was probably louder than it should have been at that hour.

"Rahshaan, who is that with that voice sounding like a drowning cat getting stabbed in the ass?"

An old lady came around the corner into the living room. She was tiny, cute, and that same dark brown shade as Banger. "You say hello to someone when you come into their house."

"Hello," I responded in a flat tone. I wanted Banger to like me, but I had to make it known that I wasn't going to kiss his family's ass.

The old woman looked at me like she didn't have a minute of her time to give me. Banger introduced me to his "G-Ma" as his friend. She asked how long he planned on being friends with me. That lady didn't seem to like me from the start, but something about her made me feel comfortable and welcomed.

I asked him again if all of the kids were his, and he told me that he didn't have any. All of the children in that house belonged to his cousins, aunts, uncles, neighbors, and neighbors of friends. Banger said his relatives just dropped kids off for his grandmother to watch. Every now and again, they came back for them. He told me helped his grandmother get them ready for school every morning.

They all fell in line with the little system he had worked out for them. It was the grossest thing I'd ever seen. Five at a time they crowded around the sink brushing their teeth, while one of them took a shower. The showers lasted no more than five minutes before he banged on the wall for them to let the next one in. He gave them all lunch money and a little something extra to get something from the corner store after school. No matter how many more kids came in, he had enough money for them to eat and get a treat. He lined them up and sent some of them to a bus stop with someone who was waiting for them and put the rest in cars with the Geno's Auto Sales logos on the sides. The shit was like a shelter.

By the time he was done, it was eight. I had exactly one hour to get ready for work and school. I hated rushing, but I pulled it together. He offered to pick me up after class and take me to lunch and work, but I already had plans. Then, he asked if he could come scoop me that night.

"Nah. I got the photoshoot. Probably won't be done until late, and I gotta study and do homework after that."

He nodded, grinned, and told me that my ambition turned him on. I wondered why he didn't try to hit if he was so turned on.

Best picked me up from school that night. He'd been on the waiting list for being my boyfriend since the eighth grade, when he saved up his picture taking money to buy me a bouquet of daisies. He was a cute brown boy with a baby face, a red Honda with red tinted windows and rims. He always had good weed, but he wasn't anyone I'd want as a boyfriend.

We went up to his apartment and got done with the pictures quicker than usual. He seemed like he was in a rush to fuck, because he didn't even try to spark one before he started kissing on me. After what I had the night before, his kisses bored me. He had an outstanding head game, though, and that was the real reason I kept him around.

"That's not the same guy you were with this morning, Monaysia," my mother nagged me when I walked into the house. That woman turned into a vampire as soon as I came home from college. When I was in high school, she went to bed at 9pm sharp every night and didn't wake up until her alarm went off at six. During those days, Best would steal his parents' car and take my friends and I all over Sanford County, only staying out of South and West Sanford.

"I'm aware, Mother."

She sucked her teeth. "Well, since you wanna be a smart ass, where is the check that you promised me the other night? Light bill is due soon, and you being home made it go sky high."

I couldn't believe she was really going to make me part with my money. I thought she'd want me to save it since she expected me to pay for college on my own. I huffed and puffed and asked her how much she wanted.

"You should sit down and do this with me. We need to figure out one third of all the bills."

I huffed and puffed again. "Can I just write you a check for a thousand dollars?"

She blinked at me several times. "You make that much money?"

"Not really, but I have that much in the bank, and I'm willing to give you that much just to end this conversation."

"Monaysia, the reason why I'm doing this is to teach you how to be fiscally responsible. How can you do that if you're just throwing money at me without even thinking about how much it is?"

"Because I'm making career moves that'll make it so that you're the last person I have to give money to again," I told her. "I hooked up with some girls at school, and we're about to get our own money."

My mama's green eyes glowed. "You're gonna start your own modeling agency? I knew you'd finally tell them white people to kiss your ass and show them what real beauty is!"

I skipped over anything I wanted to say and took my checkbook from my purse.

"Now let's talk about the way that you've been carrying yourself," she pressed while she watched me fill out the check. "This having one man pick you up in the morning and another dropping you off at night has the neighbors talking."

While I wondered why everyone was peeking over their picket fences to see what Monaysia was doing, I scraped my feet on the floor. That was something I had a bad habit of doing when I was gearing up to say something my parents deemed disrespectful.

"Mommy, I'm grown, so you really can't expect me to answer any questions about who's picking me up and dropping me off."

Mommy craned her neck backward. "What do you mean I can't ask who's coming to my address?"

I looked at the floor and scraped my feet some more. "I mean, as long as they're sitting outside instead of coming in, you really can't say anything to me. Plus, I'm nineteen, so..."

"Nineteen is old enough to have your own apartment, since you want to have people thinking I'm running a whore house!" she snapped.

After the way I spent my weekend, the word whore felt like a kick in the stomach.

"The guy who just dropped me off was Best. You remember him from school," I said.

Mommy pursed her lips and rolled her eyes. "That boy who started a business taking pictures so that he could be around you at all times and do whatever you say? If he's back in the picture, then I know he's about to bankroll whatever little ideas you cooked up."

A couple of weeks passed before I heard from Banger again. I hung out with Melinda and hoped she would bring him up, but she didn't. Instead, she talked about how much money she was making. Writing my mother that check to shut her up was a great feeling, but I didn't want to touch old white men to do it. Melinda told me that all of her clients weren't old white men. She told me she could pick which jobs to go on; she just chose them by the dollar amount instead of race. With the protections she was given, she never worried about anything but her money.

That point got me thinking. "Melinda, how much do Banger and them make off of the money that you work for?"

She tugged at her ponytail. We were sitting in a sports bar close to Downtown Sanford. She was drinking a Corona. I had to go to work later to do some overtime, so I just had soda.

"Well, what you got paid that day was just your tip. They pay the people who coordinated the jobs first, and then that money gets distributed amongst everyone. Which reminds me..."

She took an envelope out of her purse and slipped it to me. When I peeked inside, she had to catch me before I slid to the floor.

"All of this just for getting in bed with a man and letting him grab my knockers while he slept?" I exclaimed in a whisper.

"After taxes—"

"Taxes?" I repeated.

"Yeah. We gotta put the money in the pot to take care of the hood. Gotta take care of what the government ain't taking care of, make sure the kids got after school programs and shit like that," she said.

"Why is that *my* responsibility?" I asked.

"Because everybody eats," she answered. "Anyway, after that, the muscle gets a fee of like 10-15%, based on the amount of work that had to be done and miles they had to drive, plus an hourly wage, just like regular security guards. Then, we get paid the rest after about two weeks."

I ran over some numbers in my head. "So I could get one of them to take real good care of me without having to pretend I like fucking dirty old men?"

Melinda leaned in closer. "One of who?"

"Banger. Squeak. Shondell. One of them. That's where I could get the most money for the least effort, right?" I sipped my soda, waiting for her answer.

She cracked up. "Girl, get your own money. Them getting broke off for protecting you is the best way to go, because women in this line of work get raped, robbed, or murdered. Keep your relationship with them on that level. Don't go chasing them niggas' pockets. It ain't worth the headache."

"So why'd you call me and ask me to go on a date with Banger that night then?" I wondered.

"It was just something to do." She shrugged. "He showed an interest in you, and I ain't never seen him show an interest in any chick beyond wanting to fuck her, so I thought it was a cute way to wind down, especially after the way I set you up.

"Don't get caught up with them niggas, though. They might be good for an orgasm and getting a bill or two paid, but they'll have you fighting bitches over them and all types of shit. You see how Squeak treats his baby mama. You don't want that to be you, do you?" Melinda flagged down the waiter and ordered us some wings.

I contorted my face into disgust. "That could *never* be me. I wish a nigga would tell me to ask somebody for their leftovers."

We both cackled so loud that people sitting around us gave us dirty looks. That just made us laugh louder.

She smiled at me like she knew something about me, and I hated the way one side of her mouth curled.

"So you feeling Banger, huh?"

"He aight. He cool," I told her.

"Well, he has been talking about you nonstop since that night. Calling you a hustler and a dime, telling everybody that he bagged a model." She shook her head. "That boy is a whore, though. He might as well get paid the way we do. Now, I'll admit, if you give him some, then your fridge will never be empty, your lights will never get cut off, and your car will never be out of gas, but as far as you thinking you hooked him? Never that. You'll never be the only one."

My brows shot upward. "You know this from personal experience?"

"Girl, no. I been working for them niggas way too long and seeing them do too much shit to ever get caught up with one of them. They're sluts. All of them." She changed the subject. "What's really up with you and my brother, though?"

I shrugged. "He's just something to do. I'll never make him my main."

Melinda cackled again. "Look at you. Got a taste of that long money, and now you too good for these little niggas out here with their small change."

I wasn't sure if she was trying to bait me into saying something bad about her brother so she could run back and tell him, so I didn't say anything. That conversation told me I might have to watch her.

We watched a couple come into the restaurant. The man was a couple inches taller than me with pouty lips and wavy black hair with a shine that matched the chain hanging down to his crotch. The girl threw her hips when she walked, looking down her nose at everybody. I glared at her. She smirked at me and fingered a gold nameplate that announced her name was Monique, but the guy she was with bucked his eyes at me.

"Hola, Nay-Nay."

The girl he was with shot him a nasty look while he sent her to a table. He came to me.

"You miss me?" he asked.

"Where is my money, Miguel?" I demanded through gritted teeth.

"I'm flipping it. Give me some time, and I'll have you exactly where I promised you," he told me. He grinned at Melinda. "Don't I know you from somewhere?"

"No," she snapped.

"But aren't you the one my brother—"

I grabbed his arm. "Leave her alone, Miguel. I want my money, and I'm not playing with you."

He caressed my face. "Let me make a few moves, and I promise I'll get it to you."

"No, Miguel, I want it now! You told me that if stuff didn't work out in The City, then you'd be here for me. I need you to—"

"Monaysia!" Melinda growled at me. "Don't ever let me hear you begging a nigga for shit, least of all a nigga from West Sanford. All they do is steal, lie, kill, and destroy."

Miguel smirked at her. "Who would know better than you?"

He bopped away, leaving Melinda shaking.

Giving my parents that thousand dollars only made them ask when they could expect the next payment. With a smug expression on my face, I laid enough money to cover the cable and phone bills for the next two months on the kitchen counter fan-style. They asked when I'd include the light bill money.

As I stomped up to my room, I wondered what was going on with their finances. I checked the news to see if the bus companies were laying people off or if the financial planning industry was going extinct. We'd lived in the same white and green house with the white picket fence and two cars in the detached garage for as long as I'd been alive. That thing should have been paid off nineteen years later. They shouldn't have been struggling, but every single thing was about money at that point in time. Their money problems could not become mine.

Even though I had no plans of going in on any more bills with my parents, I wanted to keep my bank account cushioned. My weave was starting to get busted, and I didn't want to go back to buying hair that came from a pack. Melinda was right: I got a taste of that long money and didn't want to go back to the way I lived before.

"What are you doing after work tonight, Monaysia?" my dad asked me as I got ready to leave the house the next morning.

I turned to him. "I wanted to see about getting a car with the money I've been saving. Do you have time to take me?"

He nodded and smiled. "I knew getting you to pay some bills would propel you toward full independence. I'll take you to get a car after work."

Mommy eyed both of us but didn't say what was on her mind.

Best picked me up for school that morning. He took me to get breakfast at McDonald's, but I didn't really want it. He made a face at me while I picked at the food in the parking lot.

"You getting sick of me again? You only like McMuffins when you like me," he remarked.

I shrugged. "I haven't really been hungry since I came back home. My parents want me to chip in on groceries, so I just trained myself not to get hungry anymore. I gotta get my weight down before I get back to The City anyway."

Best cracked up at that. He was so cute when he was happy. His teeth were so perfect and white.

"Yo, you be wildin! You ain't gonna eat if you gotta pay for your own food?"

"Why would I pay for food in my parents' house? I don't pay for it anywhere else, and I've been eating at five star restaurants more than I've been eating from their table. They owe me some meals if you ask me," I said with my nose in the air.

"What if they're having money problems, Monaysia? People don't usually just refuse to pay for their kids' college education." He tried to reason with me while he changed the CD in his car's stereo. "Forever Always" by Monica played before he spoke again. "And your sister is in college too. They're probably going broke putting her through that."

"So? Why is that my problem? They should have saved like they always tell me I need to do." I was really irritated with money being a problem when it didn't have to be.

Best pulled out of the parking lot and headed toward SCC's campus, slowly because of the layer of ice on the roads. I hated how quickly New York's weather changed. When I checked the temperature in Paris that morning, it was 68 degrees and sunny.

He chuckled and shook his head. "You need to stop being a brat and help your parents out. They might just be trying to teach you a life lesson. What if something happens to them? Then what are you gonna do for survival?"

I reached out and touched his light brown face. I ran my hand from his cheek to his neck. "You ain't gonna take care of me?"

"Can you survive off of Egg McMuffins every day?" He started laughing, hoping I would join.

I didn't, not when I could cross the bridge for crab cakes and the best Chablis in The County.

We walked into the Bethune Student Lounge, where the news played. That TV was always locked on Channel 3 per some agreement with the school. I didn't mind. My idol, Hope Thomas, was on, looking flawless. I had to get my look book in that lady's hands. If I could get something I designed on the news, then I could get people to take me seriously again.

"Why can't you just take your book down to Channel 5? Them homely old hoes can use all the help they can get," Best said.

"Nope. Hope Thomas is the most watched, and you see why. Nobody's badder than her. She's been on the news since I was a little kid, and she's only aged backward. Her body's only gotten better." I stared while commenting on the ebony-skinned woman on the TV.

"People say everything that comes out of her mouth is a lie, though," he pointed out.

"Who cares when she looks like that?" I asked.

Best's pager went off. He looked at the screen.

"This is probably about a job. I'll see you later," he told me, and tried to kiss my cheek, but I dodged it. He knew better than to make people think we were together in public.

"Ask whoever it is if they know how to get me near Hope Thomas so that I can put my lookbook in her hands," I told him as he walked away. His strides lengthened as he studied the number. The closer he got to the phone booth, the more his walk turned into a bop.

"How do you know it's that type of job?" he asked.

"Because you doing the money walk. I see you!" I called after him, causing the students within earshot to laugh at us.

He shook his head and laughed. "You just be ready to work, moneymaker. I got some big things happening. Thanks for coming back home to be the face of them."

I really wanted an SUV, but I settled on a Mitsubishi Diamante. It was a cute pearl color. My dad put me on his insurance, but I wrote him a check for my part of the six month premium to give me one less headache to deal with every month. Then, I had to get snow tires, which was stupid, because why didn't a car I bought in the middle of October already come with them? It was obviously winter by New York's standards. I was mad as hell when I got done paying all that money, so I just sat up in my room for the rest of the week and wished for someone to rescue me.

By the weekend, I was still mad. Even though the money for Saturday's party flyer came with a bonus for a club appearance, the final payment didn't do anything more than piss me off. My mom came into my room while I was rushing to finish a paper. The smile on her face was enough to take the edge off my irritation.

"Look who's here!" she sang and then stepped aside. All my girls were there. I hadn't seen or heard from them in weeks. I missed the hell out of them. I went to them and hugged them.

Yolanda pulled her golden microbraids into a bun at the back of her head and commented, "I still can't believe you go to work and school. You gotta be so tired."

"Oh girls. It's community college. It's really not that difficult to be an adult when you make adult choices," Mommy said before shaking her head and going down the stairs.

"Anyway!" I shouted loud enough for my mother to hear. "What are y'all doing here?"

"Well, me and Yolanda sang in this amateur contest at this club last night, and Miguel came in there asking about you and who your man was," Siraya replied. "He was talking about all this money he came up on for you and how you were gonna be set for life."

"The same shit he said before I left. I'm off him," I said.

"Good. You should be. He fell off. Everybody's saying he's all coked out, and he sniffed up all that money he claimed he put aside for you," Yvette reported.

"Anyway, girl. We came to see you, not see you and talk about your old baller. We wanna know what's up with you and the dude you left the club with last time we went. Who is he, and where are the rest of his friends?" Brooke interrogated. "And what's up for tonight?"

"Word, Nay. My mama said she saw you driving a new car around, and I saw Ronnie and Best hanging up flyers for a party you're doing. You came home from New York and too good to hang more than once?" Yvette asked.

We could all hear my mother cackle at that. Brooke and Yolanda laughed.

"We don't care about whatever happened down there, Nay-Nay. We're glad to have you home," Siraya said gently.

Hearing her acceptance made me exhale slowly.

"Y'all should come to the party. It's a sports theme at The Opal Lounge. Wear your cutest jersey. It's supposed to be tall heads in there. We might all get us some ballers tonight," I told them.

"Is the new owner gonna let us in? We ain't twenty-one yet, and Rashad said he acts real funny," Yvette pointed out.

"If that was an issue, do you think I would have suggested it?" I asked.

"Well, I can't afford a jersey dress. Interns don't get paid at the newspaper," Yvette complained.

I was used to getting or making them things to wear to the parties I went to, so I always made sure to work on something trendy for them whenever I started a collection. Those were my girls, and I didn't roll with bums.

My mother always tried to warn me about them never giving me anything in return. I didn't listen to her, because she really didn't seem to have too many friends. I'd had my clique since I was in junior high, and she just started hanging with their mothers after I established my crew.

Walking into The Opal Lounge was cool until they started talking about what they would have done to stay in The City. They couldn't believe I let something push me back to Sanford County. When Yolanda started talking about how much ass she would have sold, I stomped away and went to dance on the bar to get the party going. From there I could see that there were more guys there than girls. My whole crew could win if they'd just shut the hell up.

While the DJ played songs by Juvenile and Jay-Z, I had the crowd chanting the lyrics and watching me pop my booty like it was paying the rent. I pulled down my Buffalo Bills jersey dress while I hopped down from the bar. Rashad had a drink ready for me. I asked him why he didn't have a whole setup for my girls.

"Not this conversation again," he groaned. "Nay, shit has changed. The new owner sits in the back and watches every single person I give drinks to. I can't lose this job. I just had a baby. And I can't let my baby's mother hear I was giving Siraya free drinks, since I used to talk to her.

"When?" I exclaimed.

"You better ask your friend about how bad her judgment was while you were gone."

I sipped the Bacardi and stood in my denial. I screwed my face and started to turn away from him, but someone stopped behind me and blocked my way. That person was way too close and getting ready to get cussed out.

"I got her, Rashad, even if she is a wack ass Bills fan."

My free fist clenched. Anyone who knew me knew I was all about the Buffalo Bills. My dad used to take my sister, Kidra, and I to their games whenever he drove the bus out there during our childhood.

"Rashad, what kind of people does your boss let in here?" I asked.

"Quit acting brand new, and turn around."

Banger. I was starting to think I wasn't going to see him again. I made sure to press my knockers against him when I hugged him and kissed his cheek. The crisp, clean scent of Coast soap came from him. I wanted to scrub him with it every day just so that I could sniff him. A nutty smell came from his braids. Every woman within a 20-foot radius looked at me like she wanted to be me in that moment. He was looking damn good until I saw he was wearing a Cowboys jersey. We frowned at one another's choice of team. An outline of the definition of his pecks could be seen. Even without gold chains like the ballers and dope boys wore, he still grabbed more attention than anybody else in there.

He asked me who I was with. I told him I was there with the same friends, and he told me to ditch them and come with him. He kept looking at my legs exposed by the short jersey dress but making smart comments about the team until he saw how upset I was getting about it. Then, he apologized, asked for another hug, and asked me to leave with him again. I told him I couldn't leave them stranded. Somehow, he talked me into giving my keys to Yvette and leaving Rize with my friends while I left with him. Rize locked in on Siraya and took her into a corner to feel her up.

"But why won't you ask your friend where the rest of his friends are?" Yvette suggested, looking up at Banger and then behind her at Rize.

"Just answer the phone when I call you to bring me my car, and don't run out all my gas." I gave her my back while she told me once again to ask Banger if he had a friend he could introduce her to. The way Yvette begged for attention from men was embarrassing. Getting away from her was the best thing for my nerves. I was glad when the door shut behind us.

Banger led me across the parking lot. People heading toward the door groaned at my departure. I shouted assurance to them that the party was still going. Maybe someone would go in there and show Yvette some attention. It would be nice for her to stop acting like she never got any.

"Oh you bought a car. That's why I ain't heard from you," Banger noted as he held the door open and helped me into a Lincoln Navigator.

"If you wanted to see me, then you know where I live and how to dial my number. You must have been too busy for me."

He didn't have a response to that. He just drove, his hand on my thigh as he headed into the Sanford metro area. I was glad he didn't take me to that creepy river. He took me to another restaurant that I'd never been to and asked me if I had made any steps toward getting back into modeling. I told him that being on the party flyers was the only progress I made.

There was so much sympathy in his eyes as he listened to me over dinner. My heart and soul really felt cleansed by the time I finished whining. He pulled his chair around the table, put one arm around me, one on my bare thigh, and told me he couldn't wait to see me back on top.

His hands barely left my body after that. Our next stop was a hotel close to Downtown. We smoked some more of that potent weed that knocked me on my ass the first night I met him. My conversation with Melinda came back to me. It was kind of a joke at the time, but I started to wonder if every night with him would be like that night?

I blew a shotgun into his mouth. He took the smoke in slowly and then slipped his tongue into my mouth. I gently bit down on his bottom lip and sucked it. This time, he wasn't leaving me with soaking panties and hard nipples.

When we pulled away from each other, he got up and turned on the TV. *Midnight Love* was on BET. Usher was singing "Nice & Slow." He started walking back to me but stopped at the edge of the bed. It had been a long time since I had someone that sexy standing over me. I pulled him toward me to kiss him again. After our lips touched, I pushed him back and yanked off his jersey. That gave me the chance to get a good look at him. He was built like he was a boxer by day and bench pressed couches for fun. His shoulders looked like they could carry all of my problems, and his hands looked like they could crush everybody who caused them. Not even Miguel looked that good shirtless. I had to make him mine.

"Shorty, what you doing?" he asked when I tugged down his boxers.

"Getting what I want before you try that gentleman shit you did last time," I told him and gobbled down his dick. It would have choked me if I had a gag reflex. He let me suck him off until I felt his legs tensing. Before he busted, he flipped me over. His teeth lightly bit down on my nipples. Feeling his mouth and breath all over my skin drove me crazy. He stood over me with his eyes locked into mine and stuck his fingers inside my pussy. It had been forever since somebody besides me rubbed it that good. I tried to pull him down on top of me, but he grabbed both of my wrists in one hand and pinned them above my head.

"Relax. I been wanting this for weeks."

I exhaled and watched him push the rest of his clothes to the floor. He ran his hand down his dick just long enough to let me see what he was working with. He penetrated slowly and held it there to let me feel how long and thick he was. We stared at each other. An enticing confidence was in his eyes. When I was able to exhale, he sucked on my bottom lip and took in my breath.

That was the last gentle thing he did to me that round. He pulled my legs up over his shoulders and plowed into me. The fresh scent of his soap met with his woodsy cologne and barreled through my nose the exact moment he hit my g-spot. My eyes and mouth were stuck wide open. A smirk was on his lips when he realized he was in the perfect place. I was trying to dig my nails into his back to keep me grounded, but he kept repositioning himself so that I couldn't. That was fine. I didn't need to mark my territory on the first night. He was never giving that dick to anybody else after I got my turn to show him how I did.

"Damn your pussy good as hell!" he grunted. "You gonna cum for me?"

"I already did," I moaned when he took a long, deep stroke.

As he shook his head, he told me, "You ain't cum hard enough for me."

My legs trembled above my head. He hammered into me until I yelled over LSG singing "My Body." It felt so good. I thrust back, matching his rhythm. His eyes bulged when I clamped my muscles around his shaft. I dug my nails into the mattress so hard that one broke.

He kissed me and told me, "Them shits was ugly as hell anyway. This pussy got me wanting to take care of you from head to toe."

When he pulled out and commanded me to ride him, I thought about my conversation with Melinda again. It was a weird time for her to keep popping up, but I made an executive decision when I climbed on that dick. I squatted over him and held nothing back. We were already irresponsible enough to have started that without a condom. There was one way that would guarantee me never having to pay my own bills again.

He flipped me back over to the missionary position. His sweat dripped on me. I opened my mouth and drank it. Then, I pulled him down closer and licked from his collarbone to his neck. He pulled away slightly, probably scared that I was going to try to give him a hickey. I didn't need to leave marks on him, though. I was pumping back until

I got into his head, and all he could think about was how I threw this pussy at him.

He announced that he was about to nut. His hips pulled back from mine, but he cussed while his eyes rolled backward. I pulled his face close to mine and tongue kissed him again. We sucked in each other's moans. He pulled away again. The act of him moving away with so much ease was a total turn-on. My legs quaked. He scooped me off the bed and hoisted me against the wall. I locked my legs around him and snatched his hand so that he knew I wanted his fingers in my ass while I orgasmed.

"Your pretty ass ain't that freaky," he remarked when he pumped back into me.

"You scared?" I challenged, and then moaned when he stuck two fingers inside. My body went limp for a moment, but then I dug my heels into his legs. He grunted. I pulled his face to mine and gave him one long tongue kiss that lasted longer than his grunting and his body jerking. My juices ran down both of our legs. He let me down slowly.

Afterwards, he asked me if I could stay with him for the rest of the night. I couldn't move. When I was finally able to get up to go to the bathroom, my legs felt like they were going to melt into the floor.

I damn near had to crawl to the shower and back. The nigga had the nerve to come get in the shower with me and hammer me again. That time, there was no foreplay, but there was twice the amount of passion while he pulled me to him by my hips and gave me those deep strokes that made my legs wobble.

I waited hours for him to bring up the fact that he nutted in me all four times that we fucked that night, but he never did. The most that he talked was during sex where he told me how well he was going to take care of me. As I laid on the pillow top mattress, I couldn't wait to hold him to his promises.

Before we left the hotel, I called Yvette and told her to meet me at my house with the car. She asked me if I could get dropped off at her house instead. I agreed without thinking anything was weird about that and skipped behind Banger to the Navigator. That sex had me on another planet.

On our way into the restaurant, he asked me if I was still single. I thought about how much I should have told him about Best, who I'd probably be seeing that night.

"Yeah, I'm still talking to a couple of people. I'm not really looking for a boyfriend, so..."

He cut his eyes at me and stopped walking. People behind us huffed at his hand on the door, but he paid them no attention. "Why don't you want a boyfriend?"

"I guess I do, but I don't feel like hearing a nigga lying to me about stacking money for me to start my business just to sniff it all up," I muttered bitterly.

Banger opened the door and put his hand on the small of my back while we were led to our table.

"That's what your last man did to you?" He scooted toward me in the booth and put an arm around me.

Him touching me had me ready to go back to the hotel, but I played it cool and asked, "Why do you care?"

"You said you don't stay single long. I'm tryna be next up," he told me. "So that's what you want from a nigga, just help you out with getting your modeling started again? What you need? Lights? Cameras? Sewing machines? Unlimited fabric?"

I smiled at him.

"You grinning and shit. I'm serious. Ain't no reason why your sexy ass should've had to leave The County to go beg some white people to accept you. Them bastards can't see what perfect is when it's standing in front of them, then fuck 'em."

That wasn't the first or last time that anybody said something like that to me, but his tone and the look in his dark eyes made me believe he would get whatever I told him I needed as soon as we left the table.

"I can't ask you to do that for me. If I do, then you'll be so busy hustling that you won't have time to spend with me," I said.

"You ain't been fuckin with the right niggas, shorty. Real niggas know how to handle business," he said.

"And how is that when every other nigga I fucked with said he had to hit the block to get me what I want?" I asked.

"You asking questions when you ain't answer mine yet," he said.

"Well, I got a photographer. The sewing machine and fabric is a nice start, but I need yarn, knitting needles, crochet hooks, a storefront, somebody that knows how to make catalogs, somebody to pay my bills to keep my parents off my back while I'm working. It's just a lot. That's why I gotta finish school, get these degrees, and make six figures. I'll probably be too old to model by then, so I'll just concentrate on this fashion thing. I'm way more into making clothes than I am taking pictures."

"Your parents are on some bullshit," he told me.

Our pancakes being delivered to our table ended the conversation. I tried to pick it after we leave the restaurant, but he demanded that I stopped talking in his car. I asked him why. That seemed to piss him off, so I went through the CDs in the car but didn't find any Monica.

My stomach started turning when we pulled up to Yvette's house. The temperature was like forty degrees, yet she was standing in her front yard. I figured my car must have been parked in the garage since her parents only had one car to go in it. I started walking up the driveway, and Yvette's dumb ass followed me without speaking. Banger was still parked out front, waiting to make sure I pulled off okay, I guess.

"Your car ain't here," Yvette finally said when I put my hand on the garage door's control pad.

I turned on my heels. "Then where is it?"

She started picking her nails and fumbling around with her words.

"Bitch, where the fuck is my car?"

My car was at an impound lot, because it got totaled when Yolanda crashed it while driving drunk. I gave Yvette the keys specifically, because she was usually the most responsible. Yolanda had already crashed her mother's car and two other family member's cars while sober. She had the nerve to be drunk in mine? Oh hell no!

"Why the fuck weren't you driving? I gave you the keys!" I hollered.

"That bartender asked me to go home with him, and he didn't want to wait for me to drop Yolanda off, so I gave her the keys to make sure she had a ride home," Yvette replied.

I wanted to punch her in her sharp ass chin.

"So why didn't you just give the keys to Siraya or Brooke?" I kept pressing her.

"Because Siraya was with the only nigga you put any of us down with, and Brooke was off doing her thing. Yolanda was right there. Don't be acting like it was okay to just leave us at the club."

"Girl, please. The only reason why y'all even came to see me was because you knew I could get you in that party." I stomped down her driveway and back to Banger's Navigator. "You got time to take me somewhere?"

"Not really," he grumbled. "I gotta get to work soon. Why? What up?"

I told him the short version of the story, putting some of the blame on him for making me leave my car with them. He huffed and puffed about having to go to a police lot, but he agreed to give me a ride, grumbling that he'd made me a promise that he would be more dependable than my ex.

I didn't expect to cry when I got to the impound lot, but I bawled like a baby when I saw that destroyed front end. I hadn't even had that car a whole damn week.

Banger just stood there watching me have a tantrum.

"That shit was ugly anyway. Just take the insurance money, and get some new shit."

I wanted to fight him for being so casual, but I had to save my energy for Yolanda. That bitch had something coming to her. At the impound, I told them the car was stolen from a venue the night before, and that I fully intended to press charges. Banger went to the Navigator and locked the doors while I stood, bare legged, in that tiny jersey dress and dealt with the police. Banger didn't say a single word to me after that. His jaw and eyes were tight the whole way back to my house.

The gate was open when Banger pulled in front of my house. My parents were standing in the doorway. Banger just pulled off wordlessly. I was too heartbroken over my car to care about him, but my parents looking at me like they had a problem let me know my day was about to get worse.

"Where is your car, Monaysia?" Daddy demanded before even opening the door.

"It got stolen last night," I whimpered. "I went to the impound, and it's wrecked! Why do bad things happen to me when I'm doing good things for people?"

Daddy gave my geyser of tears a look of disbelief. "Siraya has been calling both your phone and our phone all night, trying to get in touch with you. You gave the keys to someone who was irresponsible in the past."

We argued the semantics of the situation, insurance premium increases, and whether or not this was any of my parents' business. As always, the conversation went back to how much I embarrassed them. I went into the house and paged Banger 911 to come back and get me. He was talking all that shit at breakfast about my parents, so he should have put his money where his mouth was. He didn't text me back, though, so I ignored my mother saying things like "last strike" and "final warning" and called the insurance company. Mommy could just hold her complaints until after I filed my claim.

"Nay-Nay, that's real fucked up that you called the police and told them Landa stole your car." Brooke couldn't wait to give me a piece of her mind over the phone. "You shouldn't have dissed us like that for that cat. Who was he anyway?"

"I just wanna know if his friend is really single," Siraya chimed in on the three way.

"Yes, girl. Dang. His whole crew fine and paid. Stop acting so thirsty," I told her just to shut her up. "Y'all some ungrateful bitches. You got into the club for free, free custom made outfits, got a ride to the club without having to give up gas money, drank for free, met cute dudes, I made sure y'all had a way to get home, and y'all couldn't even bring my car back in one piece? I should individually whoop all of your asses myself."

Brooke sucked her teeth. "Nay-Nay, stop it. You sound serious, and I ain't about to play with you like that. What you need to do is call the police and tell them what really happened. It's bad enough that she got a DUI from that cat buying us all that liquor, but you putting another charge on her, and that's fucked up."

"What's fucked up is y'all using me for my ride and connections to get into the club. Y'all disappeared on me for weeks, but pop up the minute I get a car? Y'all must think I'm stupid."

By the end of that conversation, the enemy lines were clearly drawn. I was going to have to beat Brooke's ass and Yolanda's ass. Nobody was going to pay me back for my car, because, apparently, it was my fault for showing my friends a good time. So much for being nice.

It didn't dawn on me that Banger took personal offense to my issue with Yolanda until he didn't return my pages. I wasn't about to sweat him, though. He would be back one way or the other.

I had bigger issues on my hand, like dodging Miguel. Somehow, he heard about Yolanda crashing my car and was offended that I had accepted being back home permanently. He showed up at the next party I did at The Opal Lounge and started a fight with some guy I was dancing with. When I asked him about the money, he had every story in the world but wouldn't accept that I was done hearing his lies.

After that, he started following me around town. My dad told me that he would put me out of the house if he found out I had given out his address to someone crazy enough to follow me around Sanford County.

The thing about Miguel was, I wasn't supposed to date him in the first place. When our parents fussed at us to stay away from those thugs from South Ridge, they screamed at us to "stay away from them crazy ass Puerto Ricans in West Sanford." We all shook our heads and wrote them off as paranoid racists. Our little hamlet sat on the outside of the point where the two met, but we weren't supposed to travel to either. What do you do, though, when they come to you?

I met Miguel while I was walking home from school one day in the tenth grade. He was so fine and brown with his drop top ride and wavy hair, and he pulled up to me speaking Spanish. I told him I didn't understand a damn thing he was saying, so he got out of the car and started whispering it to me. He was 22, and he had his own apartment. He always had good weed and liquor, and always had the nicest little gifts sent to me when I went out of town for jobs.

A little while after that, he started popping up at all my fashion shows and photoshoots. He said that he had connections all over and wanted to make sure that I got to where I wanted to be. He bought me clothes from my favorite designers, jewelry, and he even crashed my prom and pulled me out of the limo I got with my friends and put me into a Lamborghini so I could make the entrance that turned the most heads. He begged me not to go to New York City, but he was crazy as hell for thinking I was going to stay in Sanford County when the world needed to see me. He told me that he would be at home waiting for me, hustling, putting away money, and picking out warehouses for me; so that I could just start working as soon as I finished school, but he disappeared as soon as I left.

He always used to tell me that he loved me and couldn't wait to see all my dreams come true, so I was confused the first time he didn't answer my pages.

So Miguel lied, Banger didn't answer my calls, and then Melinda told me that Best had a baby on the way. I felt so lonely. That was stupid. All I had to do to get a man was stick my head out the window. But I didn't feel like being bothered for once. This was the longest I'd ever been single.

I found out that I could get birth control without my parents finding out if I got it from the student health center, so that's where I wound up one day in early November. I cringed through peeing in a paper cup and then sat in an exam room, legs swinging, studying for a Sociology exam. Melinda paged me to let me know she was outside waiting to take me to lunch. I'd started hanging with her more since my clique was obviously no more. I wanted Siraya to hang out with us, but her parents forced her into slavery as soon as they found out I was working full time and going to school.

*"...Because if Monaysia can do it, then of course you can work* two *jobs and go to school, Siraya."*

Sometimes I tried to treat Melinda to lunch, just so she would know I wasn't using her. She never let me pay for anything, though, and she took me to places all over The County. Sometimes, it was just a little sports bar. Other times, she'd call me early in the morning and tell me to make sure I was dressed for places with valet and five courses. I sat there and looked at a poster for a domestic violence shelter while I wondered where she was taking me that day when the nurse entered.

A sour look was on the woman's face when she asked if I was there for birth control or an abortion.

I screwed my face and snapped, "I wrote birth control on that paper, didn't I?"

"Well," she snapped back at me and rolled her neck in a full circle, "we don't give birth control to pregnant women."

"What the hell does that have to do with me?" I snapped back at her.

"I just ran a test on your urine. You're pregnant," she said in a flat tone.

"I just had my period, so I can't be pregnant," I argued.

"Well, I'm gonna take a blood test to confirm what I already know, since my medical knowledge obviously isn't good enough for you."

It was a cute idea when I was just frustrated with my parents, but to be pregnant by someone who wouldn't return my calls was a lonely ass feeling. I figured it was Banger's, because he was the only one I let in me raw. Best was too broke for me to not wear condoms with. Banger probably wouldn't believe any of that, but I kept thinking about how well he took care of those kids who weren't even his. I could only imagine how well he'd care about a child of his own.

But would my child really have to live in the raggedy ass Nat Turner projects? All my parents' warning about that place came back. They told horror stories about people there getting hooked on drugs, selling their babies, and then crying to the police months later that they'd been kidnapped. I'd better not ever hear about him having my baby down there. I was pissed off thinking about arguing with him over it.

Then, I realized that I needed to tell him about the baby so that we could argue about the baby's living arrangements. It was stupid of me to think that low of him anyway. That was just his grandmother's house. He drove Lincoln Navigators and made good money. This was a good move for me.

I didn't even close the car door before I said to Melinda, "If you know how to get in touch with Banger, I need to talk to him now." I hoped I sounded excited rather than panicked. The faster I got to him, the faster I could get this show on the road.

She smirked. "Not even gonna think about an abortion, huh?"

"Girl, what are you talking about?" I tried to play dumb and gripped the ceiling handle as she ripped out of the parking lot.

"You got that look on your face like the world is ending. You're either knocked up, or you got the package," Melinda commented.

"I'm knocked up," I quickly cleared up for her.

"And you're sure it's Banger's?" she sort of asked, sort of stated.

"He's the only one I didn't make strap up," I told her.

"Good."

I didn't know if she meant that for my sake or her brother's.

People bicycled across the bridge despite the low temperatures. Melinda said they were foolish enough to think it would help them avoid the police interrogation. On the other side of the bridge was

Sundown Boulevard. That was the right name for that gloomy ass street. The only block that had life on it was the one where Hair Revolution was located. Melinda parked her car in front and told me to follow her.

When we entered Furniture Revolution, Melinda was greeted with a hug by a handsome man called Chillz and a beautiful woman named Selena. Chillz had the same dimples as Lynn, but he was way nicer than her. According to Melinda, Chillz and Selena had been together for a million years but were waiting for something before they could get married. She told me that their wedding would be the biggest, most beautiful one ever, and Chillz told me to make sure that I had something nice to wear to it.

Melinda asked Chillz about Banger and Rize, because wherever you found one you would find the other. He pointed to a door in the back and then looked at me. Instead of sending us back there, he got up and got him for us.

Banger gave me the driest "What up?" when he and Rize came out the back room. His face dropped a foot, like I was the last person he wanted to see.

"I need to talk to you. It'll only take a minute."

He didn't follow me outside, and after what seemed like a million minutes, I didn't think he was going to. Then, the door finally swung open, and he stormed out.

"Is your friend still locked up?" He stepped into the parking lot and leaned against an SUV.

The space between my shoulder blades tensed from hearing him ask about someone besides me. "I don't know. Who gives a damn? Fuck that bitch."

"Because I thought that was real fucked up what you did behind a dumb ass car. You probably got a newer one since then."

"Look. I ain't come out here to talk about her stupid ass," I cut him off. "I just came to let you know that I'm pregnant, and you're probably the daddy."

It was so cold out there in that parking lot. Snow fell, but that was nothing compared to the icy wall he put between us. "Fuck you mean 'probably?' What am I supposed to do with that?"

I paused before answering. "I mean, I fuck a lot, but you're the only one I didn't make strap up, and I was purposely trying to get pregnant by you. Now I'm halfway there. All I gotta do now is wait and make sure it's yours."

The words sounded stupid as I spoke them. I wasn't really embarrassed, though. I felt confident that this was all going to work out for me. Maybe it was because he didn't choke me or punch me through a wall. I took the paper from the clinic out of my purse and held it in front of his face to prove myself. As he read it, he stared at me with the most hateful look in his eyes.

"The fuck you try to get pregnant by me for? You don't even know my real name. And you a snake. I'd cut my nuts off before I got stuck with you for the next 18 years. You all for self. I really thought I liked you, too, but I'm glad I saw who you really was at that impound. You ain't shit but a snake and a scammer."

My shoulders dropped. He was telling me off, and I stood there and took it until Melinda came outside. She she softly instructed me to get into the car. We rode to my house without her saying anything. I kept looking at the due date on the slip of paper. It was either Banger's baby or Best's.

I wasn't exactly upset, and that was weird to me, but I couldn't concentrate on anything other than how Banger said everything to me short of hating me. I'd been called many different names by many men, but him calling me a snake made me feel lower than low. It bothered me that I let a man get to me like that. I thought I'd learned my lesson after

Miguel. Somehow, Banger made me care about what he thought about me without even doing anything for me.

On the way home, Melinda told me she would take me to get an abortion. She even offered to drive me to Albany or New York City to get it done if I didn't want to be seen going into Planned Parenthood anywhere in Sanford County. I thought about taking her up on that offer. Pinning the baby on other men was pointless, because none of them could give me the life I deserved to live if I went through with carrying their baby.

I was supposed to go back to school, but I asked Melinda to take me home. My bed seemed like the best place for me. My pager went off. I dove for it, thinking it was Banger, but there was a code in it that I hadn't seen since before I left for New York City. It was my birthday, 1-28-80, followed by the day that we met, 6-9. I frowned and pushed it to the side. A message saying, "I LOVE YOU" went across the screen. I ignored three back to back texts with our code on the screen followed by 911 until I couldn't take it anymore. I called Miguel and told him I would meet him at Diamond Park a few blocks away.

"No!" he roared.

"What do you mean no? I gotta get to class, Miguel," I said.

"You can skip one day of school for me. You know I'll make it worth your time," he said. Then, his voice dropped low, and he started begging me in Spanish.

I started walking toward the park, but Miguel's silver Lexus LX pulled next to me when I was a block away from my house. I saw Siraya running down her driveway, waving to get my attention, but Miguel barked for me to get into the car. He pulled me to him and shoved his tongue into my mouth. His face was pressed so hard against mine that they could have cracked and interlocked. He ran his hands through my hair and then jumped back.

"Ooh that is *nice.* I've never seen you with hair so rich!" he commented and started stroking it.

I pulled away from him. "Stop. You're gonna mess it up."

"Who bought it for you? You've never cared about me messing it up before," he said with a smirk.

"I got a promotion at work," I told him.

"Work?" he yelled, and leaned toward me. "Monaysia, why are you working? You're supposed to be going back to New York City and getting back into fashion school and becoming a model! Why are you stuck here being regular like the rest of these bitches here! You are above these bitches! You should be getting ready to go to Milan, not community college!"

My eyes bucked, and I shrank against the leather seat with his name embossed in the headrest.

"The plan was for you to get out to New York City and get a head so big that you never came back here unless you were wearing a fur coat and carrying a poodle and getting off of a plane long enough to be the celebrity who put a star on the Christmas tree Downtown and then go right back to Tokyo, because you're too good for this place. Why are you here getting ready to go to a class at a community college?"

"You sound like my parents," I whimpered.

He jerked the car away from the curb and headed west.

"Well, for once, we agree. Why would you go back to the house of people who are waiting for you to take care of them? All of that resentment can't be good. Why do you think I haven't been around?" he asked me.

"Miguel, you haven't been around because you've been fucking everything moving. You started that as soon as I turned the key in my dorm. You didn't even come visit me like you said you would," I said.

He snarled and rubbed his nostrils. "Because I have been working. Every bitch that you've seen me with has been carrying packages for me."

I watched the street names go from being named after precious gems and metals to being named after Hispanic civil rights warriors. It made me wonder if he thought my night would end with me cooking drugs in a kitchen somewhere. He must have thought my failure made me less than the exceptional woman I was. My hand went toward the door handle, ready to hop out at the next light.

"I hope you didn't come get me to make me do it," I said when I turned my attention back to him.

He hit the brakes in the middle of traffic. The cars behind us laid on the horn before going around him. "Why would I make you do work? I don't even want you working that job you have now. You're not one of those bitches. You used to be my favorite girl. Now you're just turning into a hometown loser."

For an hour, he drove through West Sanford and fussed at me for being home. He'd never taken me to his part of the world before. There was a jewelry store in a plaza next to a Dominican restaurant he said his aunt owned. He stopped in there and picked up a pair of bamboo name earrings and nameplate necklace on a herringbone chain with a matching bracelet.

"When did you have these made?" I asked.

"When I heard you were back," he told me.

He took me to West Hills. I didn't even know that part of Sanford County existed. It was like Beverly Hills if they allowed Latin American flags to be flown over every door. Miguel's two-year-old LX almost looked raggedy amongst the BMW 5 series and Mercedes E classes parked in front of the stores and at the curbs of culs de sac we rode by en route to his destination. He stopped at a fine jeweler where he had to be buzzed in, and the sales girl greeted me by name. We were shown a bunch of different pieces, and then she brought out a ring and told me to try it on. Whatever she said about platinum princess cuts went in one ear and out the other while I stared at the ring. She took off one and placed another on my finger.

"Miguel, what are you doing this for?" I asked him.

"Because I wanted you to see what I've been doing since you've been away. You think that I've just been around town with hoes in tight jeans, and I have been working for us," he said.

The yellow gold looked the best on my skin, so that was the ring that I chose. I thought we'd go home, but he took me all the way through West Hills to a mansion in West Mountains. He said he wanted me to meet his mother finally, but only their servants were there. One of them told him that his mother was out of town, so he rushed me out of the house in case his father was home. His father, he said, was a marine and the meanest man on Earth.

So we took a shortcut from West Sanford to get to Memorial Mall in North Sanford. He told me to get whatever I wanted from Jackson's department store. I forgot about my bun in the oven and filled the bags with clothes in my current size.

When we got back to my neighborhood, I didn't want to get out of the car. Miguel had taken me on some shopping sprees before, but none were like that one. None ever ended like that one either. Usually, we'd park somewhere so that I could show him how much I appreciated him. That day, he pulled over close to Siraya's house and took one of my hands.

"I'm going away for a while," he announced.

"Where are you going?" I asked.

"Away. You're not going to understand the things that I'm going to do to get you where you need to be. It's better that you're not around it. I'll send for you when I'm ready. Are you going to wait for me?" he asked.

I huffed. "Miguel, I've been waiting for you for a year. This is the most I've ever gotten out of it."

"So you're saying I'm not worth waiting for?" he asked.

"I'm saying I'm too old for you to be playing with. Go sell another little girl these dreams. Catch me when you can give me this life every day," I said.

I expected him to scream at me the way that he used to when I would tell him I had to be home before curfew, but he didn't put up a fight. Then, I understood. I was being laid off because I was too old for him. Too old meant too smart, and he couldn't fill my head with the same lies anymore. At least I got diamonds out the deal.

I felt like I was in high school again, going through the back door to sneak my bags inside. This time, it about my parents looking at my bags and thinking a shopping spree meant they could ask for more money. I went through the back staircase and sucked my teeth when I saw my mother. Then, I looked again and saw her carrying a roll of my fabric on top of something. I zoomed in on the bags in her hands. She did the same to mine and cleared her throat.

"Jackson's had a sale, and I had a gift certificate from work," she mumbled.

"Oh. I won a gift certificate at work for the most customer compliments," was my response.

We stood there, shuffling our feet and staring at each other's bags.

"Nice earrings," she said when she finally looked at me.

"Your bracelet is even nicer," I said of the sparkling tennis bracelet she wore.

We shuffled our feet again.

"You don't tell your daddy, and I won't sweat you for light bill money next month?" she bargained.

"Deal," I said and headed up the stairs.

She reached into my bag and pulled out a skirt to put into her bag.

I turned to her.

"Your thighs are too big for this. Mine are just right. You should invest in a treadmill since you won't need to pay a bill next month," she said, and headed back toward the basement.

My phone rang off the hook when I got into my room. Siraya's parents' phone number was on the Caller ID. I also saw there were four messages on the machine. I stuffed the ring into my nightstand drawer and then answered the phone.

"Are you okay?" she panicked into the phone.

"I'm good. I just came from shopping. I got you something so you didn't think I was tryna act funny when I saw you earlier," I said. "Why? What happened?"

"I called to ask you. Miguel got pulled over in front of my house. They raided his car and arrested him. I don't know what they found, but it didn't look good," she said.

"Probably all the leftover stacks from the cash he spent on me," I said. "Girl, he got me a ring!"

"What kind of ring?" she exclaimed.

I said, "Maybe he knew he was going away, and that's why he did that. He spent so much money. Did you know there were mansions in West Sanford?"

"No. I thought it was nothing but projects like South Sanford with a bunch of Puerto Ricans and illegal immigrants," she replied.

"Girl, he took me to this jewelry store like the one all the rappers go to in the videos and movies right before they get arrested and either have a shootout with the police or do a bid," I said. Then, I got sad. "I'll drop off the shirt I bought you tomorrow."

"Are you crying?" she asked, but I hung up the phone instead of answering.

I turned on the news and watched a story about kilos of drugs being found in West Sanford. A blip about some missing kids went across the screen, and then they talked about how much money was found in mattresses during the drug raids. Miguel's face came on the screen when they announced who was arrested. I started sweating bullets while I waited for the police to come get me. My mouth filled with a sour taste while I stared at the ceiling.

The phone rang. I was scared to answer it, thinking maybe the police would call me to tell me they were going to arrest me and how

I should dress. The caller didn't leave a message on my machine. The phone stopped ringing.

My mother came into my room without knocking. "Are you sick? Did you have a date that you forgot to cancel?"

Eyes stuck to the elephants on my wallpaper, I replied, "No. Why?"

"Because there's someone downstairs asking for you. Tell these gentlemen that they can at least comb their hair before coming to your mama's door."

I sat up in bed. There was only one person who fit that description. I shot out of the bed and past my mother. She hissed my name. I stopped and looked at her.

"That's not how we do. Make that fool wait for you. I don't care if it's been a year. You never let a man know that you're anxious to see him."

I nodded my head and dragged myself down the stairs. The SCC sweatsuit I changed into hid my shape, and I wanted to change, but Mommy was right. I had to act like I didn't give a damn. I went down the stairs and into the living room where daddy was death-staring Banger from his recliner. The tiniest smirk was on Banger's face while he stared back at him. I pushed Banger out of the house before anyone could ask to be introduced.

"Don't you need to put a coat on?" Banger asked while we stood in front of my house. "What do you want?" I folded my arms and looked at him. Wild hair or not, that square jawed, cold eyed, chiseled nosed, thick necked muthafucka was fine with his dark brown ass.

"G-Ma said she had a dream about fish," he told me.

I shook my head around, shrugged, and widened my eyes. "So what?"

"So that means somebody close to her is pregnant, and you came to me talking about I knocked you up, so I guess that means I gotta step it up."

"So you didn't believe me when I came to you with a note from a doctor saying I was pregnant, but you believe your grandmother telling you about some fish?"

I hugged myself to warm up, but wanted him to put his arms around me for the body heat.

"I believed the pregnant part, but look how you came at me: You pregnant, and I'm *probably* the daddy. Okay. And?"

"It don't even matter, because Melinda is taking me to the city to get an abortion."

He ripped open the gate. At the same time, my neighbors across the street pulled their Buick into their driveway and stopped to stare at Banger with his hands on top of his head. They waved to me and asked when I was going back to Paris. I acted like I didn't hear them and focused on Banger.

"Not if that's my baby, you ain't going to get no abortion!"

I hissed at him. "Could you lower your voice, please? I haven't told my parents, and there's no point since I'm not keeping it."

"Fuck that!" He got so loud that I thought he replaced his voice box with a bullhorn. "You talking about killing my child!"

"What if it ain't yours, and the real daddy don't want nothing to do with it? Then you leave, and I'm stuck with a baby."

"What you mean 'stuck?' You don't get stuck with a baby that you fucked to get pregnant with." He stormed away from me but yelled behind his back, "Get in the car!"

I planted my feet. "I ain't going nowhere with you all mad like that."

"Get in the car, Monaysia!"

Getting into the car was a better option than answering whatever questions my parents had, so I took that one. Banger stopped at a department store in Ruby Plaza and bought me a coat, a few days' worth of clothes, and the soap and toothpaste that I liked. I thought we were going to the telly, but he took me to the projects instead. There were only a few kids there, so we slept in the bed that he said really belonged to him but was sacrificed for other people's kids. I hated the eggshell walls and clutter of that apartment. He told me he would clean it after the last child went to bed. Otherwise, there was no point.

His grandmother was one of those holy people who didn't want me spending the night, but he told her we had some things to work out. I wondered how she could tell him who could and couldn't spend the night since he paid all the bills. He told me to shut up. Then, he lay in the bed with his arms around me, hands on my stomach, begging me all night not to kill his baby. I had my mind made up by the second time his voice wavered, but hearing him beg gassed me up so bad it was dangerous. With this baby in me, I could get him to do anything. When it was confirmed to be his, there was no limit to what I'd be able to get him to do.

The following weekend, I was deep into studying for a Biology exam when my phone rang. Best was on the other end, sounding like my probation officer.

"Where you been at? I came to take you to get an Egg McMuffin three days in a row, and you ain't picked up the phone or been at the crib."

Best had never just dropped by before, so him telling me he did irked me. What if he and Banger showed up at the same time? As the years went on, he seemed more and more pressed to hear me say the word no.

"Who answered the door, my mom or my dad?"

"Your pops," he replied. "He told me he was gonna shoot me if I ever came back."

He and I cracked up at that. My daddy loved telling boys that. He didn't own a gun in the first.

Best came to pick me up within fifteen minutes. His eyes were on my nails and my shearling jacket. The new leather smell filled his car.

The normally cocky glint in his eyes dimmed against the shine of the rhinestones on my fingertips.

"You got a promotion?" he asked.

"Something like that," I replied, knowing I looked like new money.

We went to get something to eat, and then we went to his apartment. I sat on a red leather loveseat in the spare bedroom he used as a studio. He had a bottle of Remy Red and some trees sitting on the arm. He started to take the top off the bottle of liquor, but I put my hands up to decline.

"I can't drink, and don't even think about lighting that around me."

He craned his head backward. "Why?"

I smiled and crossed my legs. "I'm pregnant," I proudly announced.

"It ain't mine!" he hollered before the sentence completely left my mouth.

"It's probably not," I agreed with him. "I only let one nigga go raw in me, and it wasn't you, so don't sweat it."

He stared at me like there was something wrong with what I said. "You been fuckin other niggas?"

"When is your baby due?" I asked with a smirk, instead of giving him the obvious answer.

"How you know about that?" he asked me. "My sister told you that? I know y'all are best friends now."

"Does it make you mad that I'm cool with your sister?" I asked him. "We don't talk about you and your personal business. I heard about your baby when I asked where you were at the last party. Your baby mama is pretty. Y'all are gonna have a cute baby."

"You fuckin other niggas?" he asked me again.

I scoffed. "Best, I have always been fuckin other niggas. I'm not about to be in her position, being lied to by you. There's a certain dollar amount you have to make for me to listen to your lies. I don't even know why you're acting all surprised when you told your sister I'd be a good fit for where she works at."

He stood and hollered defensively, "I ain't told Melinda shit like that!"

I stared at him. For as long as I'd known Best, his voice got high pitched when he lied. His voice was damn near a whistle at that point.

He lowered his voice. "Aight. I could see how maybe she might could have perceived that I was insinuating that you would fuck for money when she heard me tell Ronnie you made my toes curl for some name earrings, but I ain't think that meant she was gonna take that and say that meant you were a hooker."

Something about him using the word "hooker" made me mad. It implied that he thought his sister was beneath him, and Melinda was doing way better in life than Best. I felt like I had to defend her.

"You made it sound like I was wasting my talent, so she wanted me to get what I was worth and stop messing with small change."

Best's face went from brown to burgundy. I saw his Adam's apple bob in his throat. "Have I been 'small change' when I've been taking you from work to school, and putting you on flyers, and keeping you liquored down? You ain't never paid for a drink in your life messin with me, Nay!"

"Best, be real with yourself for a second. Have you seen me? Because I have." I leaned back and twisted my body to give each of my curves a chance to be showcased in their best light. "When would I ever pay for my own liquor? And you wrote to me in school every single week about modeling for party flyers. You said your camera only acts right when I'm in front of it." I stretched out my legs and leaned back in the beanbag chair. "It sounds like you gotta learn to stop running your mouth. Otherwise, we wouldn't be in this situation."

"You keeping the baby?" he asked me, staring at my stomach. There was nothing there yet, so he chuckled. "I can't imagine you fat."

"Your sister offered to take me to get an abortion, but the nigga who I think is the daddy wants to keep it, so yeah. I'm keeping it."

I watched his eyes twitch. "You keeping a baby because a politician asked you to? What if he ain't the daddy?"

I paused at him mentioning a politician and then couldn't help but giggle to myself about the assumption he made.

"Then you'll have two babies to take care of." I looked around the room to think about where we would put a crib. For the first time, the stains in the carpet bothered me. I couldn't imagine having two babies in that one bedroom apartment.

"Hell no!" he roared. "Monaysia, you being stupid as fuck. I got a wifey."

"This is my first time hearing about her, and you've been asking me to be your wifey since 1993," I pointed out.

"That's because I would drop anybody I was with for you, but it sounds like you too flashy for me now," he said.

"I've always been too flashy for you, honey. You've just always been my sweetie," I told him, rubbing his face.

He jerked away with a frown and told me, "You need to get an abortion. I can't afford any more kids."

"You gonna pay for it," I told him. I was getting a kick out of him telling me how low budget he was after whoring me out to his sister.

"Monaysia, that's like five hundred dollars. I don't got that kind of money with a baby on the way. I don't give a damn how fine you are. You ain't gonna get me enough party flyers to pay for two kids." Something clicked in his head and cocked one of his eyes. "How the fuck am I supposed to make money now if your ass is pregnant?"

"I would hope that you and Ronnie would have shown your work to more people and got some other type of jobs by now or met some other girls that wanted to be on the flyers. I know they ain't gonna sell like me, but you can't seriously think you're gonna just be doing party flyers for the rest of your life and living off of that," I said.

"What do you think I'm in school for, Nay?" he asked me.

"I honestly don't know," I told him. "Anyway, that's not my problem right now. Either way, you need to get it together for the baby you got on the way. See? This is exactly why your sister was trying to put me down with some richer niggas." I smirked at him. "The nigga who's probably the daddy has no problem with dropping the cash."

"Then let that nigga pay for an abortion then," he told me.

I shook his head and emphasized every syllable deliberately. "He doesn't want to. That's why I'm keeping it."

"And what if the test comes back, and that ain't his baby?"

I shrugged. "Sounds like I'll have to see you in court."

"You would put me on child support?" He sat across from me, his eyes shooting lasers, mouth frowning, tone saying that was the worst thing that could happen to him. "That's fucked up. You don't even care about that baby. You ain't never gonna care about that baby with your selfish ass. You was just complaining about giving your parents money for groceries not too long ago. Wait until you see how much it costs to feed a baby."

"That's what daddies are for."

I stopped talking after that. Best was really irrelevant to this equation. After hearing Banger beg me not to have an abortion, I had a feeling that he was going to take care of the baby whether it was his or not. I asked him to take me home. He said he didn't want to.

"Why? Don't you need to go rub your wifey's feet or something?"

"Nah. I'm with you right now, so that's who I wanna be with." He kneeled next to me, kissed the side of my face, and put his hands on my stomach. "You know I ain't no deadbeat nigga. If that's my baby, then I'm gonna be there."

It sounded like a lie even then, so I was really hoping he wasn't the father. I couldn't see myself blowing up Best's pager, begging him to bring diapers and formula, give us rides to doctor's appointments, and come to the baby's birthday party.

I asked him to take me home again. He told me he wanted me to stay so that he could prove to me he was going to be a good father to our baby if it was his. Pregnancy hormones wouldn't let me leave when I should have. Instead, I stayed in his bed and let him put me to sleep.

My pager woke me up the next morning. Best made a smart remark about it being another man, but it was just Kidra. She needed money to get home from college, because our parents told her I was going to drive to Syracuse to get her. They neglected to tell her I didn't have a car anymore until the last minute. Typical.

I had Best take me to the train station to buy her a ticket and then home so that I could start studying for my midterms.

My parents made that week so hard for me. They judged me for taking the week off from work so that I could study. After I complained about that, Melinda let me stay in the fancy apartment that she lived in with Peaches and Cream. I still didn't get any studying done, because Peaches got a delivery from some man she only called her "boo". There were four crates of designer clothes, shoes, and handbags from the major fashion houses with an apology letter that she didn't get a job in Milan. In her sadness, she let the rest of us fight over everything that was in it.

On Wednesday night, after my last midterm, Melinda dropped me off at my house at the same time that a cab dropped Kidra off.

Both of our pagers went off with ridiculous messages from our mother. She threatened us that we needed to be home by Thanksgiving to help her cook. It was ridiculous, because every year she told us to wake up at five, but she woke up at three just so that she could complain about being in the kitchen by herself. Then, she wouldn't let us do anything except load the dishwasher after dessert.

"Miguel must have a new car," Kidra said with a frown instead of hugging me.

I looked after Melinda's car. "No. That's my homegirl from SCC."

Kidra's frown deepened. "You're staying long enough to make friends? Nay-Nay, please come to Syracuse with me. We can get an apartment together, go to school together..."

"You just want somebody out there suffering and bored with you," I said.

A laugh came from the back of her throat and through her nose. "Please rescue me from that dead city! You had a car! You were supposed to come get me every weekend!"

"Who said that? I do overtime on the weekends so I can get up outta here as soon as my grades let me." We went up the walkway.

The front door swung open. Mommy fussed at us about all the food she prepped without us. She pointed a rolling pin at me.

"And, Monaysia, I don't know what you did to make these little boys sniff around here like some stray dogs, but you better no have no extra people at my Thanksgiving table!" she fussed.

"Hi, Mommy," Kidra said cheerily.

Mommy frowned at all the luggage she brought with her. "So you think you're gonna occupy my washer and dryer all weekend? Well, make sure you have your sister buy you some detergent. Mine is off limits. And maybe she can introduce you to one of these little boys who come over here looking like if trouble were money. She met that one little boy and started paying a third of the bills. You should expect to chip in a fourth during the summer."

Kidra's face reddened and then froze in shock. She gave me the nastiest glare. "I wish you would think about how the things you're doing affect both of us. Every letter they've written me this semester has been about splitting bills four ways and getting ready to pay for grad school myself. What is going on with the three of you?"

I didn't know what my parents' problem was, but I hoped the baby put an end to it.

There was no nice way to put it. Thanksgiving was going to *suck*. The year before, I woke up and went to the Macy's Parade with some friends and then went to Chinatown for dinner. After that, we went to the Christmas tree lighting in Times Square. To be sitting with people who only got together because my mother threw tantrums until they agreed to her hosting every year was disappointing. But I sat at the table with two of Daddy's brothers' family, his sister's family, my mom's sister, Marvine, and her daughter, Chrissy.

As a family, we hated Marvine and Chrissy. Mommy only invited them over to show how much better than her we lived. That year, Mommy didn't get to brag about her daughter being away, living a glamorous life. She had to listen to Aunt Marvine brag about Chrissy spending the past year away at some advanced science program. I had to follow her around and take the silverware and knick knacks out of her purse that she kept slipping in while she spoke.

I didn't know the root of my parents' problem with Aunt Marvine, but Kidra and I hated Chrissy from the first time we saw her stupid face. She had a whiny voice, and she thought she was as pretty as us. While Kidra was never one for vanity, she put her foot down when it came to Chrissy and looks. She had Mommy's face, after all.

Chrissy was the same caramel shade of brown as us with the same green eyes, but she barely had a single curve on that toothpick frame of hers. She walked around telling people she was prettier than us because her hair was two shades of blonde, but she just looked a mess to us.

Dad led us to the table while Mommy continued to fuss about being the only one who cooked. One of Dad's brothers' wives offered to help her, but she said something about some mashed potatoes and went back into the kitchen to fuss at how long it took Dad to bring the bird to the table. Once all the food was finished, one of my dad's brothers started out by saying he was thankful for the meal Denise Giles provided every year.

Aunt Marvine popped her lips and said, "Come next year, when Chrissy gets her degree and purchases a home in East Sanford, we'll be able to locate the festivities there. We'll get it catered so that Denise won't have to slave away over this mediocre food."

Mommy's head rolled toward Aunt Marvine. Dad tried to intervene half a second too late.

"Now how the hell is she buying a house in East Sanford? Is her SSI getting increased? Everybody at this table knows that little bitch gets a check, and she stays out there in Abolition Town in that crazy house called Baker."

The table went silent. If anybody else knew that, their faces didn't say it. Chrissy's eyes watered while she looked down at her plate. I almost felt sorry for her.

"Denise, why would you say something like that about your niece?" Dad asked.

Then, Mommy's head rolled toward him. "Why would I let her mama sit at my table and lie about my cooking? I cook my ass off. That's why Mama left me her dining room table and all her cast iron skillets.

She knew Marvine's ass wouldn't have no use for them, and she was right. That's why Marvine lives in them overpriced houses in Midtown while we own our house. I hope Chrissy goes before you so that she don't have to worry about you not being able to leave her nothing but that row house she stays in."

Sadly, that was one of the nicer encounters between my mother and her sister. Used to it, Daddy's family abandoned making up something to be thankful for and piled their plates with food. The doorbell rang while my dad tried to diffuse the situation. I got up to answer it, snatching the salt and pepper shakers from Aunt Marvine's hands right before she dropped them in the purse she hung on the chair by its strap.

"And what you doing standing up for her anyway? Monaysia might be back at home, but at least she's in community college trying to get something going so that she can go right back to New York City. Chrissy ain't going nowhere but back to her straight jacket," Mommy said.

"Monaysia ain't going nowhere but to stand on the corner and wait for the next man with gold rims and gold labels on his condoms to come by," Marvine said. "That's probably who's at the door."

"You're right about that, because unlike yourself, my daughter knows how to get a man and keep a man. You should ask her for instructions," Mommy fussed while I continued toward the door.

I opened the door slowly and looked at Banger. My heart raced, and that felt stupid. He was looking so good.

"You can't call me back? I told you I was coming to get you when I got off work. I left messages on your machine."

I stood there and stared at him while I waited for him to get done. "It was midterms week. I had to get away from here and study or else I wasn't gonna pass."

"Oh."

Either his indifference or the scent of his brand new Timbs made me want to take him up to my room. "Melinda didn't tell you I was at her apartment?"

He shrugged. "Fuck I look like asking Melinda where you at? And what she look like reporting to me about you?" He kissed my lips and touched my belly. I quickly jumped back.

"Monaysia, tell whoever that is to come in and get a plate, or go the hell home. We're trying to eat, and you're letting all my good heat out of my house."

"I was coming to get you to eat with my family. It's about time you met them since you about to have my baby," he said.

"Oh. Well, my mother isn't about to let me leave to eat somebody else's food, so you might as well come in here and wait for me." I leaned forward and whispered, "And don't say anything about the baby. I haven't told anybody I'm pregnant yet."

"When are you gonna tell them? You already getting thick as fuck. Look at your hips." He looked down and licked his lips.

"Monaysia!"

Before he could make an excuse to leave, I pulled him into the house. His hair was freshly braided for once. That was a relief, because the last thing I needed was for him to be looking crazy in front of my family. My brain froze as I brought him in. I'd only heard his real name once.

"This is my...boyfriend, everybody." I checked Banger's reaction to me calling him that. He was stone faced.

A bewildered look flashed across my dad's face before he stood and extended his hand.

"Your boyfriend got a name?" He was talking to me but looked to Banger for an answer. I just stood there and hoped that he didn't call himself by his nickname.

"Rahshaan Bailey. Nice to meet you." He stared directly into my dad's eyes, and I thought my dad was going to combust. Mommy raised her eyebrows toward me in approval.

There was a general admiration for Banger among my cousins sitting around the table. The boys knew who he was and jumped at the chance to introduce themselves. The girls all needed napkins to wipe their drool, but Chrissy's mouth was wide open. She didn't take her eyes off of him. I felt like I was with a celebrity while he ate a small plate of food.

"You broke up with that boy who took your pictures?" Aunt Marvine asked.

"He was never my boyfriend. We're just business partners. I tried to get him to take Chrissy to the prom, but he wasn't interested." I leaned back in my chair and sneered across the table.

Aunt Marvine glowered at me. "He said I was taking you when I asked him."

I shrugged. "He got a limo for my friends, but my ex took me in a Lamborghini. Chrissy could have taken my place."

"Who took you to the prom, Chrissy?" Mommy stared at her while she awaited the answer.

My dad's sister mumbled to somebody, "Why are we talking about the prom when these girls are grown?"

As Banger listened to our dysfunction, his lip curled. He finished his food and announced he was taking me to meet his family.

"When's the last time a boy took Chrissy to meet his family, Marvine?" Mommy asked while Banger and I left. I snatched a set of silverware from Aunt Marvine just before she dropped it into her purse and banged it on the table to let Kidra know it was her turn to watch our Aunt's sticky fingers.

He was driving yet another SUV with the Geno's Auto Sales logo on it. I finally had to ask him where his own car was. He said he was saving up for a Jeep but put it on hold to save money for the baby. That turned me off. I thought that he made enough money where he didn't have to choose between the two.

We got to a decent sized, white house in North Mountains with these ugly black shutters. They looked like arms reaching out from the house to grab and choke you. The house was packed with people from wall to wall. Some of them I recognized from that weekend with Melinda. All of the men were dressed really plain in t-shirts and jeans.

He took me through the kitchen and reintroduced me to his grandmother and then to his grandmother's sister. The two of them stopped arguing about who made better food to greet me cordially, but stared at me to pick me apart.

"You the model?" G-Ma's sister, who told me to call her Big Grams, asked.

I nodded my head.

"You look like one."

She was one of those old ladies who said something with words that sounded like a compliment but tone that sounded like she was cussing you out.

We sat at a table with Banger's friends. Rize and Trigga were there with their other two brothers, Rico and Nyir. The one named Rico looked like Rize with deeper dimples, thicker eyebrows, heavier eyelids, and broader shoulders. He was so fine that I almost dropped my plate of food while being introduced. Trigga and Nyir both had pretty, grey eyes. I assumed Nyir got locked up a lot, because the people kept saying they were happy he was home and hoped he could stay this time. All four of those boys had these deep dimples that would have looked really cute on a baby.

"This the one you knocked up? I see why you went in that raw. I would've stuck my dick all the way up in that and never pulled out!"

I turned around to see who would say something that nasty, because it sounded like a girl but had cornrows and baggy clothes like a boy. That was Moosie, and I learned to tune her out that night. She stood right over my shoulder, sniffing me. Banger snapped at her to sit down, and everybody else laughed. All I heard for the rest of the dinner was how fine I was, and they understood why he got me pregnant. He never missed a chance to mention that I was a model.

An unending number of people slid into that house. G-Ma and Big Grams talked about needing to move the dinner to a bigger place next year, and then they talked about how many more people they'd be able to feed. It was said that Nyir deep fried the turkeys, and the man named Chillz made the macaroni and cheese.

The craziest part to me was that Banger and the rest of the guys were the ones who cleaned the kitchen. They yelled at a Dallas Cowboys game while they scrubbed the countertops and loaded the dishwasher. I tried my best to keep the disgust off my face. It seemed to be a Cowboys household.

I went to help load the dishwasher, but Melinda called for me to sit down with her, Peaches, Cream, and some other girls. Then, Big Grams called all the small children into another room, and Melinda took me to a room where a one-shoulder silk tank top, soft leather mini skirt with a slit going up the thigh, and patent leather boots were waiting for me.

"Banger felt like you'd want to show that body off one more time before you started putting the baby weight on," she explained, "so he told me to make sure I picked out something you'd like to show it off in. Get dressed. Let's go."

Usually, I spent Thanksgiving going to The Opal Lounge or Precious Gems with Kidra, her friend Diane, and my clique; or we lied about my age while sneaking the rest of my crew into some club in Downtown Sanford. Banger's family took over a club called The Spot and had their own VIP room in it. It was crazy, because Chillz and Selena partied right along with us. My parents would never. They said it was Chillz who built the club, and Selena designed the interior. I thought that was so cool, because they just partied like it wasn't a big thing that it was their building we were inside of.

The Spot was another hint that everything I was told about that side of the bridge was just a bunch of rumors. That club was packed, and everybody came to the door to thank Chillz for making the first two hours open bar. He was really humble about it, his smile widening every time they told him how much fun they were having.

It felt like Banger's family was ghetto royalty, even though they didn't look like it. Most of them didn't wear any jewelry except Rize, who wore a lot of gold Figaro chains and links around his wrists and one huge chain with a gold letter 'R' dangling from it; and Selena, who had an arm full of tennis bracelets and the biggest rock on her left finger I'd ever seen. It made me think about the one sitting in my nightstand back at home.

I wanted to dance, so Banger stood against the wall while I bent over and shook in front of him. He didn't move, not even a two step. That annoyed the hell out of me. I was used to standing on bars to hype up the crowd, but Peaches and Cream already had that handled while Banger tried to shrink into the wall. After a while, I got tired of him not wanting to be seen, so I plopped onto the couch in our section. He either didn't catch that I had an attitude or just chose to ignore it. That pissed me off even more.

A glance through the glass wall that separated us from the next VIP section showed me necks, wrists, and mouths full of platinum, gold, and diamonds. Someone shining saw me looking and raised his bottle of Cristal toward me. He wasn't as cute as Banger, but he was taller with a wider frame. He wrapped a stack of money around the stem of his glass as he drank from it. I looked at the bottle of Grand Krug Cuvée sitting in the middle of the table and tried to ignore him still looking at me while a woman pulled him away from his table to dance. I was irritated that the people who literally built the club were letting other people show them up. I started to regret getting pregnant by the first man with money I got my hands on.

"It's hard being out with someone so quiet when you're used to living it up, isn't it?"

Selena was cinnamon with a touch of bronze. Her svelte frame and immaculate bone structure came with such a caring person that it was hard to be irritated by her, but right then I was irritated. It felt like she was taunting me. It was easy for her to be content. Chillz had that rock on her finger, tennis bracelets on her wrists that made Melinda's look like gravel, and her man celebrated being out with her by yelling for her to come back to the dance floor.

I gave a fake half laugh. "No, it's okay."

Selena gave me half of a smile. "I've seen your print work before in the Jackson's catalog and ads. You take beautiful pictures. And your designs! I know they were rejected for being too urban — whatever that means—" she rolled her eyes and said, "—but I thought they were incredible."

That comment messed me up. My designs hadn't received a compliment from a professional since I began college. "Thank you."

"You were trying to get signed by Model Behavior, right? I used to be signed to them and was down there helping them do some work on a couple of campaigns, but I got tired of the way they talked about Black women. They even tried to put me in the plus sized category. I'm barely a size eight. That used to make me so mad because they wouldn't even look at real plus sized women."

The conversation felt like it was about to go down the same path conversations with my parents went, so I just smiled and nodded. Luckily, she was good at reading social cues and congratulated me on my pregnancy instead.

"What you over here putting in my girl's head, Mommy?" Banger asked after he pulled himself away from Rize to acknowledge me.

"Nothing. We were just chatting about her modeling and her designs. She looked lonely over here, you know, since all the other couples are *hugged up, looking like they're together*. Get it?" She winked at me. "She's really beautiful, Banger. I hope you get back into designing, Monaysia. It's time for Sanford County to show off some of the talents we keep hidden here." She smiled at us and walked back to Chillz.

I guess he got what she was saying, because he sat with his hand on my thigh and whispered to me about how good I looked.

After hours of being at a party without partying, we went to Chillz's house. Banger had a room there too. I wondered if he thought having multiple rooms around town meant that he didn't have to get somewhere for our baby to stay. The baby couldn't share a room with me at my parents' house. They'd charge it rent.

I went to look around Chillz's house to see if that was the kind of place I wanted to live. Unlike the individual themes for each room like my mother had, his house was one cohesive design. Banger said Chillz made just about everything by hand in it. After seeing the futuristic furniture and the bad ass fireplace made of stone, I hoped he would make some stuff for my baby.

The tudor's exterior didn't prepare me for its three stories with three bedrooms on each floor. There were three more bedrooms in the basement. That's where Banger told me his room was. When I got to the staircase, I went upstairs instead of down. I had to see how these people lived. It was obvious they were the type who invested in property instead of being flashy. They were my ticket out of splitting bills.

Chillz's and Selena's bedroom door was open. Dim, multicolored lighting shone over an Alaskan king bed. I imagined them laying up in it, sipping champagne all day. Maybe they even shot pornos in there, because the shower was actually in the bedroom. They had a bathroom connected to the bedroom, but the see-through shower was right across from the bed, conveniently positioned for entertainment purposes. No wonder Selena had that great big rock on her finger.

Down the hall that was heavily decorated with pictures of every single person who was at Thanksgiving dinner, there was another bedroom. The door was pulled shut. I pushed it open. The room was a pretty arrangement of turquoise and silver, but it was a little too perfect, untouched.

"Close that door!"

The way Chillz yelled, I knew never to touch that door again.

His voice turned blue and gloomy. "It's my daughter's room." He said it like he was delivering a eulogy, so I apologized and went to the room I was supposed to be in. I had enough data gathered to tell Banger exactly what I wanted our house to look like.

I went back downstairs into the kitchen. Chillz's children were passing a blunt around and talking. I loved how they were allowed to do whatever they wanted in that house without ever hearing complaints about what it said about their parents.

"...She kept it real with me, though," Banger was telling his audience.

"You see her attitude? That ain't gonna mix with your temper," Rico cautioned him.

"You see how fine she is, though? I ain't seen none of y'all niggas bring a dime like that around," Banger defended himself.

"Yeah, she a dime," Rico agreed. "She know she is, too. When them niggas in the next section gave her the eye, she gave it right back. She wanna be the center of attention. That ain't you at all."

"I gotta do right if that's my baby," Banger pointed out. "Ain't *nobody* raising my baby but me."

"What if it ain't yours?" That was Rize talking.

"It's like Chillz said: If the baby ain't mine, then I only lost nine months of my life. But if the baby is mine, and I ain't there for him or her from the beginning, then I ain't shit as a father. Either way, somebody gotta help her out through the pregnancy. I don't see none of the other potential fathers stepping it up, dropping off clothes at her crib knowing her hips is spreading by the second — mmph — making sure she's eating."

I thought they were going to call him stupid, but they all agreed with him because Chillz said it. That taught me that Chillz was their god, and everything he said was gospel.

After a while, I got tired of standing outside the room while they talked about me, so I went in the kitchen and sat down. They all stared at me like I was poisonous. I hadn't even given them a reason to hate me yet.

Banger pulled me onto his lap and put his hands on my stomach. "You staying with me tonight, right?"

The glaring intensified. I was a little bit nervous.

"I was gonna ask you to take me home. I got mad homework to do and studying for finals," I lied.

"Oh. I wanted to go cop something at that Black Friday shit. Might as well start getting shit for the baby," he said.

Rize said, "G-Ma said it's bad luck to start buying stuff before the second trimester."

"Ain't gonna be no Black Friday sales in her second trimester," Banger reasoned. "I can get the most shit for the least right now."

"Don't get a crib or a high chair!" Chillz called from the next room. "You know I already got that!"

"You need some clothes too," Banger whispered to me. "Your ass got fatter after dinner."

I let out a flirty giggle, but everyone was taken aback by the caw and snort it was made of. The odd sound broke the ice with his family, because they all stared at me for a few seconds and then howled and shrieked out laughs. Rico and Rize had no room to be that amused, because neither of them could laugh without screaming first.

Banger worked too much for me not to take the opportunity to go shopping when he suggested it. I was about to go to his room and rest for the Black Friday sales, but the doorbell rang. Something told my nosey self to stay tuned.

"Marcus is at the door," Trigga informed Banger when he walked back into the kitchen.

Banger's face fell. A little boy who looked like he was about 13 heaved himself into the kitchen with tears and bags dragging his eyes down.

"I been looking for Mommy for two days, and I can't find her." His bottom lip quivered after he spoke.

The little boy sort of resembled what Banger would have looked liked had he been shorter, skinnier, and corny. He stuffed his hands in his pockets and sat down in the seat Rize gave him.

Banger's jaw tightened. "She don't wanna be found. Let her ass go."

"But last time—"

"Last time wasn't the last time. You old enough to accept that." He took the joint that was handed to him. Nobody told him to stop being mean to the little boy or to help him find his mother.

"I just think we should go look for her before she gets arrested or something happens to her." Marcus tried to plead his case, and it bounced right off of Banger.

"When Ma wants to come back, then she'll be back. It might take her eleven years, so don't get too attached or sit at the window waiting. Now what you wanna do? You wanna stay here, or you want me to take you to G-Ma's crib?"

"I wanna go to Big Grams' crib. I haven't eaten yet," he said.

"Shoulda came to dinner instead of running around after somebody that don't wanna be caught. And answer your pager from now on. I bought that so I could find you," he told Marcus while Rize went to the refrigerator to take out a plate of leftovers someone packed.

I'd never seen anyone be so cold to a sibling. It made me mad, so I went to bed, thinking Kidra better not ever treat me like that.

In the bedroom were pictures of Banger with every member of the family. The bed was king sized and still smelled like the wood it was made out of. I fell asleep as soon as I hit the flannel sheets.

Banger shook me later. "Get up."

"Time to go shopping already?" My eyes popped open wide.

"That's all you wanna do is go shopping. Fuck you think this is? I work hard for my dough."

He climbed into the bed with me and stripped me down. I felt funny fucking in a house that wasn't even his, but he insisted that it was his house. I kept quiet anyway, but that was hard. He was hitting the right spot and wouldn't move from it once he heard a certain moan escape my mouth. I couldn't help it. I had to dig my nails into his back and bite his neck to keep from screaming. This time, he didn't move. I left marks all over his neck to let his family know I was there to stay. After we finished, he kissed my stomach and went back upstairs with his family.

My pager buzzing by my head woke me up the next morning. I knew I didn't go to bed with it out, so I couldn't figure out how it got there. A toothbrush, towel, and washcloth were at the foot of the bed. I figured that was Selena's doing. She was so motherly. A bag of clean clothes that were a little small on me but worked anyway sat at the foot of the bed.

After I showered and got dressed, I checked my pager. Best had hit me several times, but for what? Shouldn't he have been spending the holiday with his wifey? Kidra paged me twice, but I wasn't calling her back because my parents beeped me in between hers. That could have been something small like them wanting me to come home to do my share of the dishes, or something big like Mommy and Aunt Marvine had too much Arbor Mist and fought on the dining room table. It wouldn't be the first time. Either way, I wasn't dealing with them until after I went shopping. I went upstairs to learn that I was the topic of discussion once again.

"Y'all ain't never had no pregnant pussy before? You gotta try it! That shit is like a whole new level of wet! Imagine sticking your dick in the ocean, right, and it's warm. But the ocean keeps on squeezing around your dick tighter every time you thrust. That's how pregnant pussy feels."

"Yo, Chief, you wild!" Rize called out while laughter boomed throughout the kitchen. He was the only one of the boys who called him that.

"Word to me, I put her legs up and thought I was about to drown at one point, but you know you can't nut quick in no dime, so I had to pull back and make sure she ain't have nothing bad to run back and tell her little friends."

He sounded like he was trying to stop laughing. He didn't seem to laugh very much, so it was cute to hear it.

It was barely four in the morning, but we piled in three cars and went to the Midtown Toys R Us. Banger explained they had to go across the bridge to get anything decent that wasn't overpriced. Everybody with us picked up a case of diapers and wipes. Selena wanted to buy baby clothes. She said that G-Ma already told her it was a boy, but she stuck to unisex things when she saw my skepticism.

"Where are we gonna put all this stuff?" I asked Banger as we walked through the store. The closest thing to a smile that his mouth could do was on his face when he watched me pick up bottles and clothes.

"At your crib for now," he said. He picked up a baby bathtub and tossed it into the cart.

I shook my head. "I still haven't told my parents that I'm pregnant."

"It ain't like you can hide it, so you might as well tell them when you bring all this shit in the crib with you later today when I drop you off."

He marched ahead of me and started toward the strollers. He and Chillz started a discussion about them like I didn't have a say in what my baby could have.

"My baby gotta have Mickey Mouse!" I called out to them. "Mickey Mouse everything!"

Selena's eyes glowed when I said that. With a smile, she went back to the clothes and picked out things with Mickey Mouse on them.

"I don't wanna tell them until after I take my finals. My parents are kind of old fashioned and selectively holy. I don't know if they're gonna start threatening me with needing to get married."

Banger's head whipped around so fast that I thought it was going to fall off his head. "Your pops ain't about to punk me with a shotgun wedding."

Everybody around us snickered. Maybe it was the tone of his voice that made me mad, but I was pissed the hell off for no reason. "Oh, so you could hit it raw, but you can't—"

"Don't even finish that sentence," Banger cut me off. "Whatever you're about to say is about to be stupid as hell in this situation, so stop talking.

My feelings were hurt, so I went quiet. My pager went off again. Banger shot me an all-knowing look, like somebody paging me made me less than wifey material. I flipped my hair and read the number on the screen. Then, I put it back in my pocket and stomped through the rest of the shoppers like an angry toddler. They all stopped to snarl at me bumping them. I didn't mean to make a scene, but him denying that he wanted to be with me long term in front of all those people pissed me off.

My outburst killed the mood for the day that he had planned. He abandoned the carts full of stuff that we had and went to sit in the car. Moosie pulled them over to the toddler girls' section and took a couple of the other guys with her. Chillz took down the stroller he wanted and went on about his business. Selena was the only one who stayed with me.

"Girl, I am not thinking about Shaan and his temper today or any other day," she said.

I followed her into another store. She kept holding things up to me to see if they fit. I thought she was buying clothes for me, but everything she picked up was turquoise. I really didn't wear that color too much, but there was this bad ass Laundry by Shelli Siegel suit she bought that let me know she had exquisite taste. I loved how she took her time making the men wait. She glided around like their queen. If they had a problem with it, they kept it to themselves. I wanted whatever power she had over them.

Banger got out the car when he saw us coming and gave an apology that sounded like someone forced him to say it.

"Save it," I snapped, putting my hand between our faces. I felt heat coming from him, like he was warming up his slap-a-bitch hand. He held himself back and got into the car. I heard his boys murmuring about how disrespectful I was.

"Monaysia, I think I should take you home," Selena said.

So I got into the car with her and Rize. They had some kind of secret errand to run. By then it was close to sunrise. We rode to East Sanford. I hated going over there. The people who lived there thought they were better than everybody else. The houses were nice, though. They had big yards and were far apart. They weren't closed in by white picket fences like the ones in Sapphire Cadre.

We kept going up a hill lined with Lexuses and mansions, and I wondered who they knew that lived all the way over in the Deep-Pockets District. That was the name everybody gave that place back in high school, because only the richest of the rich lived up in East Hills. We rode down the same block three times. Selena picked up her car phone and whispered for someone to come outside. Then, she drove to the corner. I felt like I should have been wearing a disguise.

A tall, dark girl with a fourteen-year-old face and my shape glided up to the corner. Rize and Selena stood behind a tree while they waited for her. She came to their side of it and handed them what seemed to be a bunch of school pictures. The two of them pressed her into a hug, and then Selena gave her the bag of mostly turquoise clothes she bought earlier along with some bags that had names like Chanel and Dolce and Gabanna on them. Rize gave her a wad of money.

I sat in the backseat of the car and wondered who she was. They had tears in their eyes by the time they separated from her. Rize hugged her like he'd never see her again. Then, she lugged Selena's gifts down the street, looking over her shoulder at them every few steps and blowing them kisses.

"That's your girlfriend, Rize?" I wanted to know when nobody explained to me what was going on. "She was cute, but she looked young."

"That was my sister, and she wasn't cute; she was beautiful." He was really offended that I called his sister cute.

"So where was she last night then? Is that whose room I went into by mistake? I thought she was dead or something from the way your dad yelled at me."

At the word dead, Selena burst into tears. That taught me to stop running my mouth. Rize yelled at me to stop asking questions about shit that wasn't by business. It was clear that he didn't like me. What was unclear to me was why I wanted so badly to change his feelings.

After pissing off Banger's entire family, I went home before I started crying about it. Since I was already feeling low, I decided to break my news to my family. Kidra met me at the door.

"You might wanna turn around and go back where you came from. It's a war zone in there." She stepped aside since I decided to take my chances.

I went through the porch and opened the living room door. My parents were yelling and throwing things at each other. We knew they had fights, but they usually kept them quiet and behind closed doors. I guessed they thought we were old enough to see the gritty parts of their marriage at that point.

Mommy threw Kidra's cheerleading trophies, my track medals, both of our high school diplomas, and family pictures at his head. Daddy yelped, shielded himself, and threw some things back. He went to her curio cabinet and started launching her knick knacks at the wall. When he started shattering the Precious Moments collection, I knew divorce papers would be on the table by the next business day.

Mommy had been collecting those Precious Moments figurines since before Kidra was born. A lot of them were limited edition. He made sure to break those first.

"What the hell is the deal?" I asked when Kidra joined me in the spectators' section against the wall.

Kidra shrugged. "They found out they were cheating on each other. Some jackass called here for Mommy a little bit after you left, so Daddy went out with some hoochie."

My head snapped in her direction. "What?"

"Where were you all night? I was blowing up your pager." Kidra moved around their argument, dodging flying objects. I wasn't as swift getting through the living room. Daddy used one of the Precious Moments figurines to practice throwing curveballs, and it hit me in the stomach.

"Ah! Daddy, watch the baby!" I shrieked, and kept going.

Slowly, their throwing came to an end while they processed what I said. They turned their attention to me.

"What baby?" Daddy demanded. He stomped to me with fury in his eyes.

"I'm two months pregnant," I told him in a plain voice. I was tired of hiding like I was in high school.

All the anger Mommy had for Daddy turned to me. "Why the hell would you do something so stupid? I thought you were trying to do something with yourself?"

"I am doing something with myself," I argued.

"Community college ain't shit, Monaysia! It's the thirteenth grade! You might as well have repeated your senior year. It's bad enough I have to explain to people that you dropped out and wound up back here on your ass. Now I have to tell people why they see you going to the welfare office and WIC. I know you don't think you can support a baby off of half naked pictures and what you make at the phone company. I've seen your paycheck stubs."

I walked away from that nonsensical talk. After staying in the house I did last night, I knew WIC and food stamps weren't things I had to worry about. Hell, even at his grandmother's house in the projects, Banger still had enough money to give the kids when the government was probably holding out, so she could just shut up.

Daddy stepped right in front of me. "Who did this to you? Was it that asshole who came over here last night?"

"Nobody did anything to me, Daddy. We decided to have a baby," I said.

"Well, where are you and this baby you decided to have going to live?" Mommy asked me. "There's no room in here."

After all the thoughts I had in my head about the house Banger was going to get for us, I still thought I had the option of staying home until it happened. I wasn't about to beg them to let me stay in their house, though.

"If I can pay for school by myself, then why wouldn't I be able to take care of a baby by myself?"

My mother snorted. "You really think community college is the same as taking care of a baby? Maybe we went about this wrong. You pay two bills and think you've got the whole world figured out." She started laughing. "Your selfish ass could never stop partying and taking pictures long enough to be a mother. Just wait until you start getting fat. You'll be too busy crying about it in the mirror to tend to your child's needs." She tilted her head and assessed the too-small outfit Selena had given me. "Looks like it's happening already. And you staying home on the weekends? You didn't think this through at all. What did he promise you? A new weave? Your nails done every week?"

"I see why you had to come home. You're a fucking bimbo." That man with those words coming out of his mouth was not my daddy. "You need to make an appointment to get an abortion, Monaysia. It's not too late to start your life again. For the third time."

I pointed at him and yelled, "Whatever woman you're screwing must have sucked your soul out through your penis, because you've never been this mean to me!"

And just like that, the argument turned back to him and my mother. I went upstairs to my room and tried to study. I had to finish college to prove them wrong.

All that talk about leaving New York made me take out my sketch pad. I hadn't looked at that thing in months. Banger had a body on him, but all he wore were white t-shirts and jeans. He was way too fine not to dress better. I started thinking of things that would look good on him. That made me start thinking of matching things we could take pictures in for pregnancy shoots and then after the baby came. Then, I heard the words "too urban" and put the sketchpad back in my tote bag.

As I sat there reading through notes, I reached down and touched my belly for the first time. My mother's words shook me, because she was right: I was too selfish for a baby. It would be cute to dress it, but diapers? And didn't they spit up all over your clothes after eating? I'd never even been around a baby to know. I damn sure couldn't be like Selena and take in his friends if their parents disappeared. What would I look like buying a house with extra rooms for children whose parents wouldn't do the same for their friends? My baby couldn't have friends. I decided that then and there.

I got lost in thinking about whether the baby was a boy or a girl, what his or her name would be, and hoping he or she had my eyes. Then, I started writing down names. I didn't want my baby to have a corny name like Edwin. That sounded like a bus driver's name. My baby needed something unique. I made a list of boys' and girls' names. Then, I chose the two that I liked the most. I kept the slip of paper with the two names on it with me for the rest of my pregnancy.

My phone rang. Best started cussing me out before I even said hello.

"I been hitting you on the hip since last night! Why you ain't been calling me back?"

"I was out and about." I pushed my books away from me and turned toward the mirror on my wall. My hair needed to be done badly.

"Oh, so you was with your first place baby daddy?" he grumbled.

"Sure was," I snapped. "*He* took me to meet his family." I went quiet to let that sit with him.

"Come on, Nay. You know my situation. It ain't no point in throwing salt into the mix until the test comes back. Me and you always strap up," he pleaded with me to understand.

I didn't care to keep the conversation going. I didn't even want him to be the father of my baby. What kind of family could he come from if his sister had to be a hooker?

"So why are you on my phone now then? Why don't we just wait until the test comes back to see if we have anything to talk about?" I drummed my fingers on my desk and waited to see what his answer would be.

"Damn. We just supposed to stop kickin it because of that? That's messed up, Nay. How long we been down?"

"Long enough for you to make me really think about being your girl!" I was yelling into the phone but had no idea why.

"You ain't thought shit like that after fucking Ronnie for a bracelet and some Air Maxes." He sat there and listened to my silence, which obviously told him that I didn't know he knew about that. "Yeah. He told me right after it happened, so I'm good on introducing you to my family. But we still got work to do before you start getting fat. Black Friday at The Opal Lounge. Let me take you to get something to eat before we do this party. I know your pregnant ass is hungry."

The word hungry must have flipped a switch in me, because my stomach started growling as soon as he said it. I wanted something with a lot of cheese and onions on it. Even though I'd forgotten all about the party, I told him to come get me.

"Where are you going now, to get knocked up again?" Daddy quipped when I walked through the living room wearing a little black dress, a tiger striped coat, and matching boots. He and Mommy had stopped throwing things at each other and were standing there waiting for someone to clean up the mess they made.

"I'm going to get something to eat," I snapped at him.

"With all the Thanksgiving leftovers we have here? That's how I know your mothering will be questionable at best. You're wasteful."

Mommy was getting ready to go on another half hour of criticizing me, so I cut her off.

"Is it wasteful if it's not my money, Mommy? It's called a date. Maybe if Daddy took you on one, you wouldn't be sweeping up your Precious Moments figurines now." My tone was snotty, but my feet shuffled like crazy while I waited for her to pick up a piece of the figurines and throw it at me.

Best's horn sounded. I zipped my coat and went outside.

"That's not the same guy who was here last night," Daddy remarked.

I kept walking. Best got out the car and opened the door for me. That was the first time he ever did that. Right before the door closed, Banger walked up behind him.

"Get out that car," he commanded.

"Who the fuck you got over here the same time as me, Nay? Damn. I wouldn't do you that dirty," Best said. He turned around and then flinched when he saw Banger. Then, he looked back at me. "You fuckin with *him*?"

"The fuck you say it like that for?" Banger looked around him and focused on me. "You fuckin' with this corny ass nigga?"

So, obviously, they knew each other. I thought Melinda kept her work separate from her family.

"Fuck this nigga," Banger mumbled, shaking his head in disbelief. "Shorty, get in my whip." Banger was talking to me like he ran things while Best was looking like he didn't want a problem. I just wanted to get into a car with some heat and close the door. It was snowing, and that bubble coat could only do so much to shield me from the cold.

My parents came outside, but Banger didn't stop ice grilling Best.

"Monaysia, you can't have this mess going on outside of our home while dressed like you're headed to a night on Hendrix or Hyman," Daddy said. "This ain't that type of neighborhood." He looked from Banger's hands to Best's to see if either of them moved toward their waists. "You have to find somewhere else to take this...and stay there." His voice cracked at the last sentence. He lowered his eyes and his head while Banger glowered at him like he was the biggest bitch on Earth. Mommy folded her arms and stood a couple of feet behind my dad to reinforce what he said.

I stared at my parents. They were really telling me to get out of their house while I was pregnant. They were scared of guns but wanted their daughter around them. How was my parenting being questioned?

Best threw his hands up. "We gotta get to work, but I ain't got nowhere for you to stay. You already know I got a baby on the way."

Banger reached for my hand and pulled me out of Best's car. "Should've just came with me to keep yourself from getting embarrassed like that. That nigga's a sucka, and them people don't give a fuck about you. Go get your books. I'm gonna help you study."

"What about this party, Nay? You just gonna leave me hanging?" Best asked me.

"I got her from here. She don't need to dance on bars for change from you no more, Picture Man." Banger kissed me cheek as he led me back toward the house.

My parents stared me down and were slow to part so I could get back into the house. Kidra went upstairs and started packing what I yelled up to the window that I needed. While Best pulled off slowly, looking back at me with shame in his eyes, my dad tried to put his foot down about what I could and couldn't take from his house. I threatened to leave and return with a police escort, but Banger told me to leave the police out of it. He stared deep into my dad's pupils and told me to take my time getting my stuff. I expected my dad to mention his imaginary gun, but he moved aside. Mommy started to protest, but my dad put a trembling hand over her mouth.

I was fucking that nigga as soon as we got into the car. That's all I could think about as I ran through my room and took whatever Kidra and I could carry downstairs in one trip. Banger came and sucked his teeth at me taking clothes when I was stretching out the slip dress I was wearing.

Kidra told me to come into her room to get the stuff she bought for the baby. Kidra didn't have any money to buy anything. She just needed an excuse to get away from Banger so she could ask me to buy her ticket back to school.

"Can I just take it out the stash in your nightstand?" she asked. "And where did you get that ring?"

"Don't go in there again, and don't tell your parents that anything is in there," I snapped at her.

"But where—"

"Mind your business. You can have whatever you want out of that room as long as you don't go in that nightstand," I commanded her.

She drew back. "Anything?"

"Just keep that nightstand locked," I told her and stormed back into my room. I went into my closet to get my sewing machine. Banger enthusiastically lifted that out of there first.

I didn't look back at my parents' house and only said goodbye to Kidra. Banger had a nice room at Chillz's house. I could see myself being comfortable there until we figured out our living situation. To get him motivated thinking about it, I climbed over the seat and gave him head all the way out of Sapphire Cadre.

He took me to the projects and said it was because his little brother was sleeping in his room at Chillz's house. I asked why his little brother didn't have his own room over there. Wouldn't it make sense to make room for both of them if you made room for one? That was another set of questions that I should have kept to myself.

We got out of yet another SUV. He apologized to me for our argument that morning. I wasn't going to mention it again, but something ugly inside of me made me drag it out.

"Is our argument the real reason why we're not going to your other house? My parents will probably be fine tomorrow. I'll just spend the night with you tonight, and then I'll get out of your way."

He stopped walking toward the brick high rise. "Who said you were in the way? Did I come scoop you, or did you call me?"

"You came and scooped me," I answered.

"Aight then. If that's my baby, then you might as well say we're together. Even though I ain't like that shit you did to your friend, I did like you before that. I was planning on making you my girl anyway."

That was Banger's relationship speed. He jumped right into it feet first and immersed himself in the idea of having a family. As I walked through the snowy parking lot with him, I realized getting pregnant was stupid. Banger was a good dude who really wanted to make up for the things his parents didn't do for him. He also pitied me because of who my parents showed themselves to be. I shouldn't have shackled him to me with that baby, but he was already off and running.

"We went back out and bought more stuff for the baby. Some of it is at Big Grams' crib. Most of it is at Chillz's. Him and Selena said we could just stash whatever we buy over there until we figure out where we're staying," he told me as we continued to walk across the parking lot, his arm around me.

I slipped an arm around his back. "So we're really doing this together thing? Wow. When are we gonna start looking for an apartment?" I asked.

"Chill. I got people taking care of that for us."

When he said that, it sounded like he had a suit-wearing financial team collecting data and creating spreadsheets, but it really meant he was watching his dollars and letting somebody who didn't know my taste tell me where I could live.

From the parking lot, we walked down an alley between two high rise apartment buildings. The only light on the alley came from the apartment windows. Light snow fell on top of what already needed to be shoveled. Banger held me up and joked about it being my last night in heels. Walking closer to the light at the end of the alley showed the outlines of teenagers leaning against the buildings. Each of them greeted Banger with enthusiasm as we passed.

Before we reached the end of the alley, a woman carrying a VCR sprinted past us. A man chased behind her, panting, calling her more variations of the word 'bitch' than I could come up with on my angriest day. I heard Banger cuss under his breath. The woman recognized him and dashed back toward him.

"Banger, get your moms, kid! She down here stealing again!" the man demanded.

"It ain't stealing if you owe my son money!" the woman taunted, her voice sounding like it came from bleeding vocal chords. "I know you ain't paid your taxes this week. We just getting our cut."

She held the VCR over her head and jogged in place. Watching her exhausted me. Her hair was thin, and she was about as big around as one of my legs. Her eyes jumped all around, looking at nothing and everything at the same time.

Then, a thought hit me: Was this nigga a crack baby? What would that mean for my child? Could you get second generation birth defects from crack?

Banger scrunched his face into a ball as he stared at her. "What the fuck did I tell you about coming down here? Quit breaking into people's houses and taking their shit."

"Come on, Rahshaan. I ain't buying nothing down here, just like you told me not to. Only ones I'm taking from is the ones that owe you street tax. I'm like the IRS for you, son." She stopped jogging and started scratching so hard that she made me itch.

"Banger, you gotta get you moms under control, man. Some of us got families that we don't want seeing this shit," the VCR's true owner said.

Now, I had no idea what was going on, but even in my ignorance, I knew that man had said something wild. I could just feel it in the air. It was like the wind blew colder, and the alley got darker. All of the people who casually stood against the building seconds before turned their undivided attention to the scene.

Banger took his arm from around me and dropped into a fighting stance. "The fuck did you just say to me, Meech?"

"Come on, nigga. Chill with that little shit. You know your moms is out of control, coming down here and breaking into people's cribs. Get her into rehab—"

Banger's fist soared through Meech's chin. I think he shattered his jaw. Meech toppled around like he was drunk. When his wobbling decreased, Banger hit him again. The man tried to swing at him, but the people in the alley rushed toward them and dared him to retaliate. Banger grabbed his mother just before she ran off and ripped the VCR from her hands. He smashed it on the ground, right next to Meech's head. The VCR door popped Meech in his eye.

"Have my money by Monday, nigga."

Banger's mom stood there laughing until he turned to her. "What the fuck I tell you about coming down here? You know it upsets G-Ma!" He turned to the audience. "Y'all ain't been serving my moms, have you?"

They all quickly assured him that they had refused her four times over.

His mother looked at me and asked, "How you keep getting these pretty girls to like your mean ass?" I wasn't sure how she looked at my stomach, wrapped up in that puffy coat, and came to this conclusion, but then she said, "And she's having a baby? I'm about to be a grandma? Look at her eyes. I'm gonna have me a pretty little green-eyed grandbaby!"

I stood there with my mouth open. There was no way that was coming around me or my baby.

"Fuck is you doing down here?" Banger roared at his mother. "I told you to never bring your ass back down here!"

She cowered like he was going to hit her next. "I— I— I—"

"Marcus said he been looking for you for two days. Why the fuck do you keep leaving him in the crib by himself? Get yourself together, Ma, and quit stealing people's shit. Some of these people actually work to get what they got." He turned to the boys in the alley and tossed one of them the keys to the truck that we'd just gotten out of. "Get Ken-Ken or PeeWee to take her to the hospital or somewhere. I don't give a fuck where she goes. Just get her the fuck from around here before G-Ma sees her."

I was turned on even more and needed to get inside to take a shower and wash my panties. He had total control over that whole alley like he was the president or something.

We kept walking to the stoop. Despite the cold, a group of boys stood out there. Their ages ranged from about nine to my age. They made comments about how good I looked and gassed my head up. He introduced me to them as his baby mama. They cheered with excitement at that. I felt like royalty.

"I remember you! You the one who bought me the chicken tenders that night when I was pregnant! How you doing, girl? I'm Shanae!"

People talked about the unique sound of my voice, but Shanae acted like she was born from a surround sound vagina or something.

"Oh yeah. I remember you too. Did you have a boy or a girl?" I asked, noticing how much slimmer her face was than the last time I saw her.

"A girl. Her name is Shanayah. You wanna see her?"

Before I could answer, she pulled me into the building and up the stairs. We went into the three bedroom apartment she lived in with Squeak and Squeak's aunt Mavis. The only thing I can say about Mavis is that she kept the tobacco industry booming. I never saw that lady without a short wig and a Virginia Slim.

The three of them needed to let Selena come in there and decorate, because that place was dark and depressing. There were liquor bottles in all the windows. They had beads hanging from the kitchen doorway like it was the 70s. They didn't even have pictures of the baby hanging up, just textured pictures like it really was still 1973.

Shanae flicked on a light in one of the bedrooms. I was surprised to see two toddlers laying in the bed before my eyes landed on the baby in a bassinet. The bassinet was the nicest thing in the whole house. It still smelled like freshly chopped wood and had a lot of white lace covering it. The baby laying inside was tiny and yellow with silky hair. I'd never held a baby before. I walked over to her and barely touched her with the tip of one of my fingers. She opened her eyes, and we just stared at each other for a minute.

"She's cute."

I didn't mean for my voice to raise with surprise, but Squeak looked like a bulldog, and Shanae looked like a Cabbage Patch doll. There was no telling what their kids would come out looking like, but all three of them were adorable.

"Thank you. You can hold her." She stood there with a cheesy grin on her face, urging me to pick the baby up.

I took a step back and stepped on a children's book. I bent over, picked it up, and handed it to her. "I don't know how. She's so little. What if I drop her?"

Shanae took the book and tossed it onto her bed. Chuckling, she said to me, "If you drop my baby, it's gonna be a problem. But go ahead and pick her up. You can't be scared. This is gonna be you in some months."

As she lifted the baby from the bassinet and handed her to me, I looked at the children piled up in the room and thought to myself that it would never be me. I wasn't doing this pregnancy shit ever again. She coached me on how to hold the baby, and I just sat in a plastic chair in the room with a baby in my arms. She looked at me like she wanted me to entertain her. We stared at each other. I sniffed the Johnson & Johnson's on her hair and skin and wanted to hold her and sniff her for the rest of the night. That powdery baby scent was surreal.

"I can already tell your baby gonna be spoiled," Shanae told me like she knew everything.

She moved around the room, picking up books, toys, and clothes. The baby snuggled against me and then cooed herself to sleep. Banger appeared in the doorway and tried to smile. Behind him was Squeak's hulking figure. He did smile and told me the sight of me holding the baby made a pretty picture. I caught Shanae giving me a dirty look over that, so I handed the baby back to her. I had no interest in being the source of an argument between her and her ugly ass boyfriend. Banger and I left to go upstairs to his grandmother's apartment.

"You looked cute holding that baby," he told me.

Was I supposed to say thank you to that? Because I didn't. Instead, I told him that I'd never held a baby before and said I never wanted to do it again. He looked at me like I was stupid.

"She was so tiny," I reasoned. "What if your baby is tiny like that, and I break it?"

He looked at me like I was even dumber. "Stop calling our baby 'it'. It's a person.

At the very top stair, he stopped walking and sat on it. Then, he spread his legs so that I could sit between them. He told me to go to

Lynn's shop in the morning to get my hair and nails done, that he'd already paid her to take care of me.

After we sat with no noise but the televisions and stereos from the other apartments filling the space between us, the heavy main door opened. The wind carried in the smell of Chinese food with it. I abandoned my past want for cheese and onions and wanted orange chicken instead. Moosie came up the stairs and handed Banger a bag of food. She winked and grinned at me. I guessed her being a girl made her feel okay with doing little bold stuff like that. Banger handed me a container of orange chicken and fried rice. I didn't mean to get as happy about it as I did, but I started dancing.

"I told you, Bro. The hoes love orange chicken," Moosie remarked while she joined us on the stairs. Soon Squeak, Trigga, Rize, and two chunky boys named Ken-Ken and PeeWee joined us. I assumed they were brothers, because I never saw one without the other. I guessed it was just a regular night to them, but I never knew you could have so much fun just sitting in a staircase and talking. My nights mostly involved liquor and getting dressed in half naked clothes. All we did was talk all night, and there was no dress code.

Ken-Ken and PeeWee should have been on stage performing or writing scripts for sitcoms. They had endless stories that kept everybody laughing. My laugh with an added snort in the middle made everything twice as funny, so it got loud in that hallway. Nobody came out and complained. It reminded me of my favorite part of New York City: it never slowed down. We listened to the wild stories the guys told and laughed until our stomachs hurt.

When there was a lull in the comedy show, Banger made me take my books out of my bag and announced that he was going to help me study. He saw my sketchpad before I could push it back in.

"What's that?" He peered at it with his hand out.

"It's nothing," I said while I shoved it back inside the bag.

"Nothing looked fly. Can I see it?"

Slowly, I took the sketchpad out of my tote bag and handed it to him. It was open to the little family collection I'd started. His face lit up when he looked at it. Silently, he flipped through the pages.

"Uh-oh, Bro. You got some competition?" Moosie guessed.

"Competition? You sketch?" I asked.

"I paint a little somethin," Banger said like it was nothing. "Maybe I'll show you later." He held up the sketchpad for everybody to see. "Ayo, check this shit out."

"That shit look just like you, Banger," Rize remarked. "She got your messy braids and everything."

"I ain't talking about that. Look at the 'fit. This shit phat, right?"

They all looked through the book and marveled at each outfit. It was the first time in a while that anyone had anything nice to say about them.

After they went through the whole book, Banger told me to take out one of my books. I took out my Sociology book, since that was the class with the most homework.

"Where the questions at the end of the chapter that I'm supposed to quiz you on?" he wondered, flipping through the section I had marked off.

"What?" I asked.

"You know what I'm talking about. In high school we had to read the chapter and then answer the questions at the end. They don't do that in college?" He turned the book upside down and shook it as though doing so would change the contents of the book.

I giggled. "No. There's a syllabus that has the questions we're supposed to be answering throughout the chapter." I pulled it out of a binder and pointed to the class's discussion questions.

He read the definition I'd written for environmental racism and then read the question, "Is it possible for environmental racism to exist in a city that is predominantly comprised of and run by people of color?"

Rize cracked a smile and commented, "Your teacher must be from this side of the bridge asking questions like that."

All of a sudden, the staircase filled with geniuses. They started by talking about how overlooked their side of the bridge was in the winter time when the snow plows were needed. I thought Moosie and Trigga were going to fist fight when they argued if that was racism or the county just not giving a fuck about poor people. Trigga and Rize thought it was the county's officials working on behalf of white supremacy, while Ken-Ken, PeeWee, and Moosie declared Sanford County was fueled by keeping people intentionally poor. Banger thought they were all related. Squeak had some conspiracy theory about the projects getting blown up one day.

Later, when I got my grades for my final, my teacher called my answer to that question the most nuanced essay she'd seen in all of her years of teaching at that college. She tried to punk me into majoring in sociology and going all the way to graduate school. She couldn't tell me how that would get me back into modeling, though, so I told her to leave me alone.

When we finally went inside, there were kids all over the place. They were all asleep, but they were like tiny mine fields to me. One wrong move could wake one of them up and cause a chain reaction. I didn't know what was up with people stuffing kids in the projects, but that wasn't about to be my life.

"G-Ma, what you doing up?" Banger asked his grandmother, who sat in a recliner in the living room. "I would've got you some Chinese food if I knew you was still awake."

"Boy, you know I don't eat that mess," G-Ma said with a wave. "I had some leftovers from yesterday, and Moosie brought me a fish sandwich from Peter's Kitchen. I ate that and sat here and dozed off waiting for Tasha to come get her baby. She ain't come, but your mama did."

"You ain't let her in, did you?" he worried.

"No, boy. You know better than that. She would've stole all this Black Friday stuff you bought for these children." She stretched, yawned, and then focused on me. "Hello."

"Hello. How are you?" I made sure to be polite that time.

"You taking care of my favorite great-grand, I hope. Looks like it's gonna be a boy." Her eyes got heavy.

"Really? How can you tell?" I wondered.

"You're prettier than you was the first time I met you. Girls take away all your beauty, but boys make your skin glow and your hair shiny. Your face getting fat, but ain't nothing else growing but them hips and that booty," she said, and then started snoring.

Banger gently shook her and then helped her to her own room before taking me to his. There were kids sleeping in his bed. He went to the closet and get a blanket to spread on the floor. It was my turn to look at him like he was stupid.

"You know I ain't gonna be able to lay on this floor once my belly starts growing," I complained. "I won't be able to get off the floor."

"Chill out. I told you it's being taken care of."

He brought his sketchpad with him. His work wasn't something I could just flip through; I had to study each picture. I jumped back at one of them.

"It's that bad?" he asked.

"You know this shit is fly," I said after I sucked my teeth. "This picture just looks kind of like my grandmother but with brown eyes. That's who taught me how to design and sew."

"That's crazy. Everybody I ever showed that picture says it looks like somebody they know," he said.

I kept looking through his work. There was a painting in the closet of his grandmother that I thought was a photograph until I stared at it for a long time. He put my little sketchpad to shame. I was in awe of that boy's talent.

My pager went off, and I guessed that killed whatever mood we were in. He took the book from me while he shot me a dirty look.

"Why you ain't never gave me that number?"

I shrugged. "You ain't seem like the type to be paging girls when you wanted to see them, so I didn't bother."

"Well you got one thing right about me," he mumbled.

The comforter under us did little to help get away from the draft on the floor. He stretched himself out and invited me to lay on his chest. Laying there and listening to his heartbeat made me feel like that's where I was supposed to go to sleep every night. His arms wrapped around me made me feel like I should wake up there every morning. A few hours later, though, his beeper went off. He wrapped me in another blanket before he left for work.

In the morning, his grandmother made breakfast for about nine million kids while they used her house as a playground. No matter how wild they got, she kept doing her thing at the stove. In under an hour, she had a table full of bacon, cheese eggs, grits, biscuits, and sausage links.

"You know how to cook?" she asked me as she made plates for the kids.

I felt like I was supposed to help, so I tried, but she just shooed me out of the way. It made me cringe when I thought about my baby deciding to have a sleepover one day. We'd be getting pizza, and they'd have to leave before breakfast the next morning. I couldn't handle all that stress.

"I can make spaghetti."

She cut her eyes at me. "You ain't gonna be able to keep Rahshaan with no spaghetti."

It was too loud to respond. When she finished passing out food, there was enough left for one plate. I started to walk away, but she fussed at me to feed the baby.

"But what will you eat?" I asked.

"Don't worry about me. My favorite grandson always makes sure I eat."

There wasn't much that I ever felt guilty about, but eating before G-Ma always made me feel bad. I planned to learn how to cook so that I could help her out.

Banger didn't get back until the kids finished eating. He had food for G-Ma and me. I couldn't believe that I was hungry again. He got the kids dressed while G-Ma and I cleaned the kitchen. Well, she cleaned. I was just in the way.

He waited for me to get in the shower so that he could take me to get my hair done. After three minutes under the weakest water pressure imaginable, he banged on the door and yelled that I had to get out. Just before I could open my mouth to protest, the water went down to a drip. I turned it off and back on, but something brown dripped through the shower head every ten seconds.

"Something's wrong with the water!" I yelled. "Call the landlord."

He and G-Ma just laughed at that.

While we walked up the alley to get to the parking lot, I asked Banger if he was going to take his grandmother with us when he moved. I hoped he didn't think all of those kids were going to start getting dropped off at my house. I had plans of strutting around in see through lingerie to keep him coming home every night. Couldn't do that around people's kids.

"G-Ma ain't never leaving that apartment, so please don't bring it up to her," he said.

I sighed out my relief, but asked him why she wouldn't leave anyway.

"She said she gotta live to see the day that place is taken care of. I don't know why she thinks anybody is ever gonna give a fuck about that hell hole, but she said it's gonna happen one day. I don't argue with her ass about it. Chillz and just about everybody else in my family has been trying to move her out of there since the '80s. You bring it up to her, and you're gonna hear nonstop speeches about the shit. Just leave her alone.

"I'm gonna go fix the water later today. I just gotta wait for the housing authority snitches to stop riding around so I could get into the basement," he told me.

"You can fix pipes?" I asked.

He looked at my thighs and smirked a little. The innuendo made me giggle.

Lynn's shop was co-owned by her and all of her sisters. The shop was never dead. There were several chairs and employees. Only the highest profile clients could get their hair and nails done by one of the sisters. Everybody else had to go to one of their protégées. The highest among the clients sat in Lynn's chair. She couldn't stand me from day one, but Banger sent me to her chair faithfully every Saturday and then to Renee's chair to get my nails done every two weeks.

"Make my shorty look good, Lynn. Don't be half assin' like I seen that chick just walked outta here," Banger called to her.

"I'll beat your ugly little face in!" Lynn called back to him. "You ain't never seen me half ass on nobody's head.

"Yeah, yeah, yeah. Just make my girl look good." He stood in the doorway. Rize came, and they disappeared together.

I swear all four of those sisters pounced on me with questions as soon as that door closed behind me. The one named Adrianne was wearing scrubs, so I didn't know why her short ass wasn't going to do her double shift at a hospital some-damn-where.

"Who your people?" Lisa asked me that standard Black ass question that I was surprised it took that long for them to ask. What really surprised me, though, was the follow-up question that I got after I told them my parents' name.

"Edwin that works at the bus station? He be at the bar on 110$^{th}$ and Hyman?"

Now, I knew my daddy went out with his friends every Friday night, but I didn't know anything about him having a "spot." I damn sure didn't believe he was anywhere near Downtown Sanford where the streets were numbered going North and South and named after singers and artists with drug problems going West. I don't mean the Melinda type of high profile escorts to politicians. I mean, "Five dollars, sucky-sucky," type hookers. What the hell would my daddy be doing in there?

"I think that must be a different Edwin that you know," I said.

"Yeah. It might be another light skinned Edwin with green eyes running around town. You never know," Lynn said in a less than convinced voice. "Can't wait to see what kind of special made Buffalo Bills jacket he comes into the bar with this year."

That jolted my eyes wide open. Daddy went to Buffalo in the middle of every December and bought us all Bills jackets.

"What made you decide you wanted to get knocked up by my nephew?" Renee asked. "Was it the car, or did he spend some money?"

"I like Banger a lot," I said. I didn't know what kind of answer that was to the question, but it was crazy that she asked me outright like that.

"Yeah, I'll bet. That's why you got mad when he said he didn't want to marry you in the store yesterday," Lynn remarked. "I heard how you showed out. He finally met his match with that attitude."

She yanked my head backward by the root. I yelped and squeezed my eyes shut to fight off the pain.

"Lemme tell you something about Shaan, though. While his mama is clocked out, *I'm* his mama. I will stomp the life outta you if you ever do anything to hurt him. Let's get that understood right the fuck now. I see right through all that sashaying and shit you do; and I'm gonna let you know that if you fuck with my family, then I'm gonna fuck you up myself. You might still got a teen behind your age, but you adult enough for me to crush every bone in your body if you ever do anything to hurt him or that baby you're carrying. Do we understand each other?"

Nodding my head wasn't good enough. She needed to hear me say, "Yes, Lynn," before she was satisfied.

"Good. Welcome to the family. Now go to the shampoo bowl and let Haddus wash and condition your hair so that I can do something with it."

I expected somebody to tell her to be nice to me, or to not put her hands on a pregnant lady, but every eye in that place was on me, glaring at me, daring me to do something wrong. Banger didn't seem like the type who needed protection, but he had a whole shop full of bodyguards ready to jump me.

Selena took me to doctor appointments. She helped me do everything clerical that had to do with pregnancy. She even came to my job to help me fill out paperwork for insurance and my 401K. I always wondered how old she was, because she looked 21 but acted like she'd been a mother for 45 years. She knew something about everything, from creating a will to pussy popping on a handstand.

She always told Banger he didn't need to come to the appointments. All he ever talked about was making money, so he seemed relieved not to have to break his stride during the day to sit in a doctor's office. He worked like every day was the last day that he'd be able to make money. The only time he came was when I had my sonogram to see what we were having. By then, he dropped the wait and see mentality and was all about us being a family. When we found out we were having a boy, he started working even more. I didn't know there was that much pussy that could be escorted around the state. Sometimes, he left for two and three days at a time. He always came back with something from wherever he visited. It was always wrapped in some sweats from whatever college was close to wherever he worked, so that was my pregnancy wardrobe.

The problem was, I had to sit up in Selena's house by myself while I waited for him to come back. Melinda offered to let me stay at her house, but Peaches and Cream didn't want anyone they didn't know that well in their house when they were gone. I respected that, but it felt like they were calling me a thief. I didn't need to steal the little hush gifts Peaches' friend gave her to keep her from calling his wife.

I called that house Selena's house, because they made it known that was who the house belonged to. One morning, she said she wanted a new dining room table. There was nothing wrong with the one we were sitting at, but by that night all the guys were carrying one inside that smelled like new fresh wood. Somebody down the street was moving out of her parents' house, so Chillz and his boys just loaded the older dining room set onto her moving truck.

Selena never cooked or cleaned. She worked at some dance studio in North Sanford and at this theater called The Green Balloon. Everybody said she made great money, but I knew she never spent a dime of it. She came home from work to a blunt rolled and a glass of Chablis poured while she waited for dinner to be delivered or cooked. Nobody bothered her until after *Jeopardy* went off, and then they would all sit around her and tell her what problems they needed her to work out. I wanted to be that bitch so bad.

They tried to include me in their family, but I wasn't interested. I wanted to get out of *that* queen's castle so that I could be treated like that in my own home. So when I was there in between school and work, I sat in Banger's room and did my homework or sketched. Sometimes I called Siraya, but she was barely ever home. When her father answered the phone that had been in Siraya's name since the eighth grade and questioned me about the South Ridge exchange that kept coming up on the Caller ID when I called, I didn't dial that number again. There was a lot of nerve over there in Sapphire Cadre.

Early one morning, Banger woke me up when he was trying to slip out of bed to go to work, so I sat up and watched the news. He gave me the dirtiest look when he saw Hope Thomas on the TV talking about the school district laying off bus drivers if their union leaders didn't come to an agreement about their next contracts. My dad was a union rep for the school district's bus drivers. I was concerned.

"We don't watch that shit over here," Banger told me in a dry voice.

"Why? She's the baddest bitch on the news," I said.

"Fuck that bitch," he grumbled.

I kept on watching her while he left and ignored his attitude. Even though he got all those kids up and dressed every morning, he wasn't a morning person at all. He wasn't a noon or evening person either. In general, he was just moody as hell. I didn't want to make any scenes that would leave me having to stay at his grandmother's house, so I just ignored his attitude.

I kept watching her talking to her co-anchor about boys reported missing from South Sanford. She kept saying "South Ridge," but the places she named were further out. I kind of wondered why she didn't know the difference, but I got distracted by the pear-shaped rock on her finger. She'd been wearing that thing for years. When I was in school, she came to career day and told us that she wasn't letting the man who gave it to her put the rest of the bridal set on her finger until he understood that she came first. I liked that.

"You know, Malcolm, I thought that these terrible reports of missing children would slow down once Jeremiah Revolution was taken off the streets, but they seemed to have only gotten worse," she said to her co-anchor.

Malcolm gave her a dirty look I was sure he thought nobody noticed, and said, "With his death sentence scheduled for next winter, Defense Attorney Joy Gilead is doing everything that she can to get an appeal. If his execution does go through, Jeremiah Revolution will be the first in New York State to—"

"Monaysia, turn that off, please," Selena said in a soft but firm voice.

I looked at the doorway and saw her holding a plate of food.

"I'm sorry, but I watch her every single morning. She is so fly, and I want her to wear my clothes on the air one day."

Selena told me, "Don't say another nice thing about that scandalous bitch in my house again."

To me, Selena sounded jealous that there was actually a woman in the world who looked better than her. I turned off the TV and didn't watch the news on that channel again in their house. It was weird to me that they allowed their grown children to bring home whatever girl they wanted but dictated what they watched on TV. Again, I wasn't interested in giving anybody any trouble without an address of my own to go to, so I held my tongue.

Selena put a wad of money on the dresser and said, "Banger gave this to me to give to you on the way out the door. He told me to tell you he was sorry he left without leaving it." She stalked away and stomped up the stairs.

Getting money from Banger was never a problem. He never let me leave the house with empty pockets. On days he was out of town, he left the money with Selena or Chillz to give to me before I went to work, even on payday. He wanted me to keep all of my paychecks in the bank and build up savings. He made it very clear that I had to spend money very carefully and work until the doctor said it was time for me to stop. Otherwise, he said, us getting our own spot would draw unneeded attention.

Everything I wanted to do would draw unneeded attention. I wanted to buy a new car. That would draw unneeded attention, and he had access to vehicles any time he needed one. I wanted to have a baby shower in this hotel my job had a conference in. That would draw unneeded attention. I wanted jewelry. That would draw unneeded attention. I started to wonder what the point of being with him was.

"Oh, girl, that's the price you gotta pay with them niggas," Melinda told me over lunch one day.

We were still cool, even though I couldn't figure out the point of our friendship. Melinda's ass was like 28 hanging out with a 19 year old. She said she really thought I was a cool person. Ain't that much cool in the world that would have me hanging with a teenager at her age.

"The police be all over them, so they make moves in silence. They ain't tryna spend no time in jail, and I thank them for that, cuz I ain't either."

I gulped down my apple juice, which was all I craved during my second trimester.

"What's the point in having all that money if you can't spend it? What would it hurt if he bought me just one tennis bracelet? All the bitches he has me around got at least three."

"Girl, you need to go live in a music video." Melinda giggled. "I already told you what it was with them. They ain't tryna get caught up like the hustlers and the kingpins. They got a whole plan for what they're doing. One day, you'll get to move out of the hood and live like Chillz and Selena live, but Banger has a whole lot more work to put in before he gets to that level. He'll get there, though. Looks like he's taking you with him. Glad you got what you wanted. I mean that. Y'all look really happy."

I wasn't happy, but people kept telling me it was the pregnancy that was making me miserable. People said I was barely showing, but I felt so damn fat. The only thing that I liked when I looked in the mirror were my knockers. They looked like some round throw pillows. Other than that, I was miserable about everything. I had one idea about what being pregnant by somebody with money looked like, and it came out another way. I was mad at myself for taking out the fetal insurance policy.

"Y'all aren't happy?" Melinda asked when I didn't say anything.

"Yeah, we are. Everything is just so corny right now because I'm fat, and I want a blunt and just one gin and juice." I joined in when Melinda laughed.

"Girl, you are not fat. Soon as that baby drops, I'm pulling up to the hospital with a jug of Tanqueray and Tropicana. Just let Auntie Mel hold the baby while Mommy drinks up.

"And speaking of aunties..."

Oh boy. Melinda couldn't go a whole conversation without bringing up her brother. "Guess who found out that he's not the daddy?"

"It wasn't Best's baby?" I said with way more interest than I meant to. I calmed my voice. "That's what he gets. He shouldn't have left that girl up in the house by herself all the time, running after me if she was his wifey."

"That's what I told him," Melinda agreed. "I mean, no offense to you. The shit was just ass backward how he never spent any time with that girl but was always chasing after you. On the low, I was happy that she had somebody else. She deserved much better than my little brother. Then again, so do most women."

The waitress brought me another carafe of apple juice. I chugged that down and said, "Well, I'm sorry he wasted his time with that one."

"He feels bad for neglecting you and focusing on her. He wants to apologize."

"I bet he does feel bad. He can apologize with cash. Other than that, I ain't fuckin' with him no more. He tried to make me get rid of my baby for someone else's, and honestly, fuck that baby. And him. He showed me everything I needed to know the night I told him I was pregnant." I tried to look at the menu and order food, but apple juice was still all I wanted.

"I understand. Keep it real, I hope your baby isn't his either. I can't see him as a father ever. He's too childish and selfish."

I wasn't sure why she told me that, so I didn't say anything.

"He only wants what he can't have and what's too good for him," she kept on ranting. "Ever since he found out that baby isn't his and that you and Banger are happy as hell, he's been asking about you. I'm still stuck on how he just let you leave with another nigga, though. Like, he didn't even try to check up on you. He's just letting some nigga take care of a baby that might be his, and I don't respect that at all."

"Why are you so mad about it, though? He's doing what most niggas would do." That attitude only came about because I was so content with Banger.

"Because that ain't how we was raised at all. He should have let you stay in his spot when your parents put you out. He claims he's had a crush on you since the 8th grade, but he ain't done shit to get you at all."

By the time Melinda got done with her rant, I was mad at Best too.

After eating, we headed to the mall for a photoshoot. By the time we got there, I'd forgotten about Best. My focus switched to convincing myself that pregnancy wouldn't get in the way of catalog modeling. We went to Jackson's Department Store, where we met with the general manager named Tisha. She was a snotty little woman, but I liked her because she always had some man bringing her food back when I worked for her through the Naomi Iman Modeling School. While I got ready for catalog and ad shoots, she taught me the value of keeping an ugly nigga in our side pocket.

She frowned at my jewelry and my belly and asked, "Shouldn't you be on the cover of *Harper's Bazaar* by now? You did all those hair magazines in high school just to wind up back here and pregnant? By one of my nephews, no less?"

I sighed and told her that she sounded like my parents. I tried to tell her about how I was treated.

"They treat all the newbies like that. It's hazing. Were you listening to me at all before each and every show you did for me?" she fussed. "I'm going to call your mother."

I was happy about her saying that as she stomped away. My mother couldn't stand that lady. My mother hated all women who found themselves attractive, and nobody thought they were finer than Mrs. Tisha Darnell. I couldn't wait until my mother told me what their conversation sounded like.

Then, I remembered my parents had kicked me out of the family. That was the first time I'd missed them since it happened.

I got so caught up in the feeling of missing my parents that I didn't see someone flying across the mall to jump on Melinda. The girl's screams broke me out of my thoughts and sent my hand straight to my purse for my butterfly knife.

"You the one supposed to be fuckin Trigga?" the girl hollered like her head was on fire. Both of her fists were clenched at her sides, and her teeth were bared like a rabid dog.

Melinda put her hand in the girl's face and strutted by her. The girl kept on screaming. "And you need to go to the clinic! He burned me, and I'm sure he got it from you, you dirty ass hooker!"

I ran up to the girl and went to cut her. My knife touched her skin, but Melinda snatched me away.

"Get your pregnant ass on before Banger cusses me out for having you out here in some stupid shit." She guided me away from the screaming girl.

"Wash your pussy, you dirty hooker!" The yelling continued as we walked away.

Melinda's hands shook when we got back into her car.

"That's exactly why I said to you what I did about them niggas. Hopefully, Banger will prove me wrong," she said, and drove me to Chillz's house.

Missing Mommy must have conjured her, because she paged me and asked me to come over. It had been about five months since I'd seen her or heard her voice. I asked Melinda to drop me off at my parents' house, and she told me to page her when I was ready to go back home.

Mommy sat in her normal spot on the loveseat when I walked into the house. She got up and hugged me, rubbing my belly with a smile on her face. That reaction surprised me.

"I'm still mad at you, but all I ever hear is how good you look and how good that boy takes care of you. And, Monaysia, you're so beautiful pregnant."

I skipped over asking who she knew who saw me to know anything about me. Instead I said, "I look like a Treasure Troll, Mommy. Stop playing."

We hugged for a long time. I sat in Daddy's recliner and looked around. "What's different about the house? Did you paint?"

"Your father paid somebody to do some scalloping on the ceiling before I kicked his ass out."

Mouth agape, I leaned forward. "What?"

"Me and Edwin are getting divorced, Nay-Nay. I should have told you earlier, but I was mad at him, mad at you, and mad at Kidra because she wouldn't give me anything to be mad at her about." Her eyes moistened. "Twenty-five years, just gone like that."

"Because of the scalloping?" I asked.

She snorted a laugh. "The scalloping was the last straw. He was a coward and didn't want to be married anymore, but didn't want to say it. So he kept doing shit to get on my nerves. He argued with me about every bill, but then I came home and saw he paid somebody to do that mess to my ceilings. It was just a real stupid way of telling me he didn't want to be here anymore. He acted like he had somewhere else to go, so I pushed him out there."

She took a tissue from the box on the coffee table and dabbed her eyes with a little more drama than was necessary for what she said next.

"After you left for The City, I was very excited. I kept waiting by that phone for you to call and say you'd met some man who was going to move you to a house in the Hamptons that had a separate house in the back just for his mother-in-law. I was mad at you for coming back because that meant I would never get out of here, away from Edwin and his constant nagging about the bills.

"Up until you got your scholarships, I never paid a bill in this house. Then, all of a sudden, Edwin started asking me why I couldn't pay a bill if you could pay for your own college. My mother always told me that the only reason a man wants to split the bills is because he wants to spend your half on some whore in the streets."

My eyes enlarged as my mind flashed back to the day that I learned my father had a reputation in the bars in the most questionable part of the county. Those sisters never mentioned it again after that day, but I always felt like they thought they had one up on me because of it.

Mommy concluded, "I guess we were just tired of each other. I didn't care that I was spending time with this other man. I looked forward to him filling my time until I got that call from you saying I didn't have to come back to this house with Edwin nagging me about my half of the mortgage. Since we didn't have to hide things from each other, we didn't have to pretend to like each other anymore."

She was trying to play tough, but she was quivering. Tears threatened to pour out of her eyes. "He wants you to call him. I left his number and address pinned to that board in the kitchen for you."

I got up and carried my weight over to the loveseat so that I could sit next to her. We embraced while she cried. When her tears dropped onto my arms and hands, I cried too.

"Do you still talk to the man you cheated with?" I wondered aloud.

"Not as much, but he makes it worth my while when I do. He's rich," she answered me.

"Good girl," I said and rubbed her shoulder.

Mommy wiped her eyes and asked, "How are you doing? Where are you living?"

I fumbled around with my fingers and shuffled my feet.

"I'm good. It's a boy," I told her while I rubbed my tummy.

"Oh that's gonna make Edwin so happy," she said. "I'm happy too. I never gave him the boy he claims I promised him. I don't remember promising him anything but Kidra. You just snuck in there when I got drunk one night at a Betty Wright concert. A boy's gonna be fun, though. Let's go shopping."

"I would love to, but Bang — I mean, Rahshaan — has already taken care of everything. I don't even need to have a baby shower."

"No baby shower?" Mommy damn near hollered. "Oh no. Kidra and I already planned one for you. You have to let us do this, Nay. Please?"

"Okay, Mommy, but I'm telling you that we don't really need anything," I insisted.

Banger's family had filled that basement with enough stuff to open a daycare.

"And please don't buy a crib. Rahshaan had one specially made, and it is perfect."

"Well, he'll need one when you bring him over here," she pointed out.

"You're gonna let me bring him over here?" I asked. "I thought you were ashamed of him?"

"You embarrassed me after I dropped that bomb about Chrissy being in the looney bin. I thought I really had the big joker, and everybody in Sapphire Cadre was gonna know that Marvine's a liar. I was so pissed at you for giving her something to gloat about," she explained. "Just because I put you out, though, doesn't mean that you have to ignore me when I beep you."

"Mommy, I've been busy with work and school," I said.

"You're doing both while you're pregnant?" she asked.

I shrugged. "Rahshaan works around the clock, so I just put up my checks for a rainy day."

"Girl, you're living my dream, it sounds like," she said with misty eyes.

"It ain't all that. We stay with his people right now. They got a nice house with a lot of room, but I'm ready for my own spot. Plus, Rahshaan's gone all the time," I said.

"Why? How long could working at a furniture store have him away?" she asked.

I wrinkled my face at her.

"Just because I put you out doesn't mean I'm not gonna check up on you to make sure that you're still alive," she said. "I had a bad feeling about him, but the best I could hope for was that he was taking care of you. I heard he was doing okay for himself down at that furniture store," she said.

"Well, that's not his only job," I snapped.

"I know that."

"He works security too," I said.

She peered into my eyes. "And where else?"

I frowned. "Why are you trying to get information out of me?"

She shrugged. "If you don't want me to know your boyfriend is one of those drug dealers down in South Ridge, then you don't have to tell me. As long as he's keeping it away from you."

"Mommy, he does not sell drugs," I told her.

"Well, Edwin did some snooping—"

"You and Edwin need to not worry about me. You put me out. I'm being taken care of. That's all that needs to be said. Now stop telling people my boyfriend sells drugs. I've never needed to be with somebody like that before, and I won't start now."

Then, I had to take a look at what happened. Banger got up every morning, busted his ass until late at night, and made sure I had everything I needed. He didn't have to work more than one job, but he did so that he could work on getting me what I needed. All he wanted me to do in return was carry his baby. I needed to be more thankful for him. The only thing the people who turned their backs on me had left was the will to get into my business and tell it wrong. Finally, I was able to see why he was so stuck on keeping his life quiet. If everybody talked the way my parents did, he was going to jail for real.

Seeing that I was pissed, she offered me something to eat to make peace. I asked her for apple juice, and she poured me a tall glass of it. After two more glasses of apple juice, we went back into the living room. I waited for her to make a comment about needing to pay her back for drinking so much of it. That never happened.

"I'd like to meet your boyfriend's parents," she told me.

I shuffled my feet around and picked at my nails. There was no way in Hell that woman in the alley was coming anywhere near my mother.

"Well, Rahshaan was raised by his grandmother, so I'll invite her to the shower. His aunt and uncle that we stay with now will come too, and so will his four aunts."

"I'd really like to go to them and see what kind of people they are on their own turf, you know?" Mommy said.

"They live in and around Nat Turner."

I knew that would shut her up. When Mommy left the projects in North Ridge after college, she took my grandmother with her and never looked back. She cringed at the thought of even driving by housing projects.

Mommy squinted at me. "You aren't living down there, are you?"

"Please," I said while I rolled my eyes. "We're looking at a couple of places, but I think we narrowed it down to the condos in Midtown."

It felt stupid lying to my mother even after she put me out, but what was I supposed to tell her? We couldn't move until God told us the police weren't looking?

Mommy frowned and shook her head. "Midtown's overpriced and pretentious. You might as well come back this way and move into Diamond Estates. At least you'll have a moderately priced townhouse or apartment with a playground nearby."

"Maybe," I said with a shrug. "It really depends on what we can afford. You might be right about Midtown. I think I heard they have to pay for parking, and the parking is on the street. That just sounds like a bad idea."

Mommy's smile grew. "Nay-Nay, this little visit with you has me feeling really good. This boy and this baby have you growing up. You're going to make a terrific mother."

Before Melinda came back to pick me up, I went back up to my old bedroom to get a few more things. I unlocked the nightstand and made sure the ring was still there. It was untouched. I moved it down a drawer and locked every drawer in that nightstand before taking two older sketch pads and my good fabric scissors with me.

"Please come over more, Nay-Nay," Mommy said when I came back downstairs. "I didn't mean to isolate you. I love you."

"I love you too, Mommy." I hugged her tight.

She walked outside with me and frowned at Melinda's car when I opened the gate.

"That's not the car he picked you up in last time," she said.

"Oh that's not my boyfriend. That's my friend from school. We're on our way back up there for our last class," I explained.

Mommy stared a little harder and then jumped like a lightbulb turned on in her head.

"Something came for you." She went into the house and quickly returned with a stack of my mail. "Looks like your check came from Yolanda's accident."

I was excited about getting my own car again, but Mommy was busy frowning at Melinda.

"Your friend certainly seems old for college," she said with her nose in the air.

Melinda looked at my mother and looked away.

"I'll see you later, Mommy. Please tell Kidra I said hi if you talk to her before I do." I missed talking to my sister.

"Your mother looks really young," Melinda said when I got into her car. "She's really pretty. You look like her."

Melinda's windows had dark tint. I doubted she could see much of my mother's face through them.

"Thank you," I said, wondering why she cared anything about my mother.

Melinda stormed into Chillz's and Selena's house and screamed for Trigga to get into her car. He crept into the kitchen and looked at her with his head slightly bent.

"I said get into my truck! You know I do not be yelling like this in Chillz's and Selena's house!"

Trigga didn't move. Melinda stormed outside. Trigga looked around for someone to help him.

"I've been paging your ass since yesterday. At the very least, you're gonna give me a conversation!" she yelled as she stomped out of the house.

Trigga zoomed in on my purse.

"Is that blood?"

Banger, who had been sitting at the table fighting sleep, followed Trigga's line of sight.

"You got in a fight?"

I looked at what they were looking at and scoffed. "This face don't get into fights. I had to cut somebody who tried to jump on Melinda in the mall."

Trigga huffed and dragged himself outside behind Melinda.

"Ain't nobody touch you after that, did they?" Banger asked. He stood and put his hands over my belly.

"That's old news. Listen. The insurance company sent me the check from my car getting totaled," I said, unable to stop smiling about having that much of my own money.

"Your ass is happy for once?" Lynn asked as she came through the door. "That's a fuckin surprise."

I didn't know why she was his favorite. She was so mean.

"Put that money up. We're gonna need it for the baby," Banger instructed me.

"But I don't wanna put it up. I want you to take me to get a car tomorrow," I told him.

He returned to his seat and said, "Ain't nobody buying a car tomorrow. That's unneeded attention."

"Put it like this: I'm buying a car tomorrow whether you buy it for me or not," I told him.

All of Chillz's sons (minus Trigga), Moosie, and Shondell were moving around the counter, preparing side dishes. The smell of apples hit my nose. Chillz grinned at me and announced that he was making pork chops with an apple glaze. That was supposed to make me smile. He'd been on a mission to get me to eat more since I'd replaced my meals with apple juice. I was too distracted by wanting a car.

"Nay, don't start with me today. I'm tired as fuck," Banger said, rubbing his face. "What you need a car for right now, anyway? Was I late picking you up from school or work this week or something? Why you need to spend money every time you get your hands on some?"

He sounded like one of those men in Lifetime movies who didn't want their wives to have a way to escape them.

"What if I want to go somewhere by myself without you knowing where I'm at?" I shouted. "I've been under lock and key since you and me got together!"

"Lower your voice in my brother's house," Lynn commanded me.

I rolled my eyes at her. "Sorry if I ruined the ghetto Huxtables, but I need my own ride."

"For what? You and Melinda get around just fine," Lynn shot back.

"Auntie, chill. I got this." Banger's eyes drooped as though he could have fallen asleep mid sentence. He turned his attention back to me and said, "It ain't that I don't want you to get around, but you having a car with no permanent address looks suspect as hell. Just chill, and trust me to take care of things. I promise we'll have everything we need before the baby is born."

Melinda was on a spending rampage and took me to Geno's Auto Sales to buy a car. The salesman seemed confused by our presence. We probably looked too high class for what we bought. I only had a third of what I paid for the last car to work with, so I had to settle on a dingy ass tan Ford Taurus.

I didn't even want the damn car, but Banger made me so mad telling me I had to wait. Who was he to make me wait for anything? He wasn't even sure if he was the father of my child. What was I supposed to do if he wasn't? Catch the bus home from the hospital? I had to look out for me.

"Whose car you driving?" Shanae asked me when I pulled up in front of G-Ma's high rise that day. Banger had paged me and told me to meet him over there that night. I had a feeling that meant Chillz and Selena needed a night off from my yelling.

"Mine," I said with my nose in the air as I walked up to the stoop to join her in the spring air.

Shanae turned up her nose at my answer. "Why you buy that? You ain't like the red Maxima Banger bought you?"

"What red Maxima?" I asked.

"Oh shit. I wasn't supposed to say nothing. He was gonna surprise you with it at your baby shower this weekend. I wasn't supposed to say nothing about that either, so act like you don't know when we get there."

I stood there feeling stupid. Everybody else was driving Honda Accords, but he was putting in extra work to make me stand out. All I had to do was wait. I sat there and waited for my brain to stop sizzling while Shanae and all the boys on the stoop laughed at me.

"You must got voodoo in your pussy. I don't understand you being the first one to lock Banger down and be so ungrateful about it." Shanae bounced her baby on her knee while she spoke. I couldn't believe how fast that baby grew.

"That's because you can't sweat these niggas, girl. You already know that." I flipped my hair, barely recognizing the voice that was coming out of my mouth. "What is hooking him getting me anyway? I gotta sleep on a floor in the fuckin projects tonight. The rest of the time, I gotta sleep in a basement. And I gotta ask him if I can spend my own money. I'm the only bitch in the hood with a job. What I look like asking permission to spend my money on me?"

Shanae shook her head at me. "You so young-minded. I understand you wanna be flashy. I do too, but that ain't what we do. We gotta look at the bigger picture and keep our money on the low." She called out to her other two kids to get away from the street. "Maybe you'll be more grateful once you see everything he's building for you and the baby, but I don't understand you. I heard you got him going this hard for you when you don't even know if the baby is his or not."

"It ain't like it's a secret. I told him when I got pregnant that it's *probably* his. He's the one who took it this far. You can't blame me for jumping on that... Not that I know what I jumped on. I could call the other nigga who might be the daddy right now and be pushing his shit and staying in his crib. He got a red Honda with red tint and his own address."

Now why did I throw in that last lie? Something about Shanae always made me have to take an inch to a mile.

"Then go to that nigga, and quit wasting my brother's time!"

Rize came through the alley, looking like he wanted to slap me. Shanae smirked at me, while the boys on the stoop continued to laugh.

"You don't deserve that nigga!" Rize continued. "My brother hustles his ass off to make sure he can give that baby everything his pops ain't give him, and every night you come in the crib to complain about what he ain't doing for you! I keep telling him to leave you alone and just focus on the baby if it's his, but he ain't gonna see 'til it's too late."

Shanae's son asked to be taken to the bathroom. Shanae fussed at him to wait. Rize picked him up and stormed inside with him, shooting dirty looks at both of us as he passed us.

I felt like Shanae set me up, so I got up and went to my mother's house. I paged Banger and told him that I was staying there for the night. He told me he wanted me to come with him, so I started an argument to get him off the phone. That was a mistake, because Mommy followed me around the house and asked me how long I was staying. She had a date with some Lexus-driving man with a deep voice. I went into my room and closed the door while I checked on my ring. It was still there. I put it on and wondered what happened to Miguel.

While I stared into the stone, a familiar number came across my pager screen.

"Long time no talk," Best said in a friendly tone after he picked up on the first ring.

"What is there to talk about? You left me at the curb to go be a family man. Congratulations, by the way." I held back my laugh.

"Quit frontin. I know either my sister or Siraya told you the DNA results," he said.

I frowned. "I haven't seen or heard from Siraya. Where did you see her?"

"I gave her a ride to school one morning when she missed the bus," he answered, then quickly changed the subject. "Can you get away from your boyfriend? I still owe you for the pictures you did for the flyer."

I drove to his apartment. My pregnancy hormones let him talk me into spending the night. I didn't plan to listen to his apology, but I did. I didn't plan to let him eat me out, but I did. I didn't plan to let him fuck, but I did. Oh well. At least he had his own apartment, and I could be as loud as I wanted while he made me nut.

In the morning, Banger paged me to let me know he was coming to get me from my mother's house. I sped over there and waited for him.

"I'm about to be late for work," I fussed at him when he got to her house.

"Call in today. I wanna spend some time with you. I missed you last night."

Now I knew good and well that Rize and Shanae told him about the scene outside of G-Ma's house, so what kind of setup was this?

"Well, that's fine. I gotta talk to you anyway. Look out back."

He looked out the window at the Taurus and then back at me with disgust.

"What the fuck did I tell you?" he growled. "Why did you buy that ugly ass car?"

"I told you why," I told him with a shrug. "We spending time today or not?"

He stormed out of the house. I ran outside and followed him in my car. The power steering on that thing was abysmal, and I was pissed. I kept my foot on the pedal and stuck to his tail while he ripped out of Sapphire Cadre and then crossed the bridge to get back into South Ridge. When he got to Sundown Boulevard, he turned left down Strawberry Fields Boulevard. I wondered who the hell he was going down there to see that early in the morning. He kept going like the police weren't a thing and went to a leasing office in the Frederick Douglass Housing projects.

"What bitch you coming down here to see?" I yelled when I pulled myself out of my car.

"Don't drive like that with my baby in your car ever again!" he commanded me, stomping forward.

I waddled after him, pissed off that the waddle was all I could do.

"Banger, don't walk away from me!" I warned him.

A cranberry Maxima pulled near us. I saw a woman in it before she beeped the horn. I ran up to it and slammed my purse onto it.

"Get out the car, bitch!" I hollered and went into my purse for my butterfly knife.

"Monaysia, chill!"

Banger's voice was so loud that every door in the area opened to see what was going on. I ignored the audience and went to snatch the door open, swinging my knife.

"Oh I'm a bitch?" Lisa challenged me while she got out of the car.

I felt stupid and wanted to back off, but she kept coming toward me.

"Auntie, she ain't know it was you!" Banger rushed to shield me from her.

"That bitch looked right at me, Shaan!" Lisa yelled. "She knew who the fuck I was!"

"Auntie, you can't whoop my girl's ass! That's the mother of my child!" Banger hollered at her.

"You don't know that shit! She told you that might not even be your baby! You doing all this shit for that bitch, and you don't know what the fuck she be doing when y'all ain't together? You think all them other niggas she was fuckin just disappeared?" Lisa yelled.

I froze, wondering if she knew anything about where I really was. Had Melinda found out and snitched on me?

"Nay, get your ass in the car," Banger commanded.

"I ain't getting in shit," I told him.

"Oh, you ain't?" Lisa ran around him and swung on me. Her fist came so close to my face that I knew she missed on purpose. I looked at her, and there was a light in her eyes that was almost as bright as the smile on her face. She got a delight from clenching her fists, bending her knees, putting one foot slightly in front of the other, and leaning all of her body weight into her swings. She was looney, and I would try to stay away from her for the rest of my life.

A man tore out of the leasing office and pushed Lisa backward. She kept a diabolical smile on her face while he lifted her into the air so that none of the punches she threw at me would land. He fussed at her about always fighting while she was on the clock. She kept swinging and kicking as though he wasn't even there. The man grunted while he struggled to get her away from me.

Shondell bolted out of his house in slippers, basketball shorts, and a tank top. A bunch of high school-aged looking boys ran out behind him. Moosie and some girl wearing lingerie on top and gripping a pair of sweatpants taut to her waist ripped toward us to help get that demon lady off of me.

"Auntie, that's our nephew she's carrying," Moosie said, pushing Lisa back gently while everyone else surrounded me and took me to the car Banger drove.

"Don't put her in my shit. She got her own whip," Banger grumbled.

Someone took me toward the Maxima, but Banger told them to put me in the Taurus. They all looked at him and awaited an explanation. Banger turned away from them, shaking his head. I turned to get back into my car but saw someone in it.

"Leave my radio alone, you crackhead bitch!" I screamed. "Don't touch my Monica CDs either!"

Banger whipped back around. "You had the nerve to put some beat in that shit?"

I heard people laughing at me from every angle.

"Miss Mary, leave that shit alone! That's Banger's whip!" somebody yelled.

Whoever Miss Mary was yanked the radio out of my car and ripped down the street.

"Banger been talking about getting a Jeep forever. He ain't settle for that ugly ass car. Not after he came around here bragging about knocking up the model. How he gonna keep a model with that hoopty?"

The high school boys ran after her, but she was long gone with my radio and two of my CDs. A group of girls stood in the doorway of the house Shondell just came out of, cracking up at me.

Lisa stopped trying to fight me long enough to ask, "Why the hell did I hide this car over here if she already bought one?"

Banger sucked his teeth and handed the keys to the truck he was driving to somebody.

"Take this shit back to where it gotta go. Auntie, take that car back to Geno when you get a chance. Tell him to give me whatever for it. I don't need it," he said.

"Shaan, you worked your ass off to pay cash for that car," Lisa pointed out.

"Fuck that car. The shit I do ain't good enough." He walked to the Taurus and opened the door for me.

"Um... What the hell are you doing?" I demanded to know. "If you bought a car for me, then we're riding home in the shit you bought for me, not this raggedy ass bucket."

And then the cycle of Lisa trying to fight me started all over again. We were out there for an hour before Banger tried to leave. When the power steering issue kept him from pulling off, he screamed one long cuss word.

"Fuuuck!"

"This is why you need to let me keep that Maxima," I grumbled.

"Monaysia, shut the fuck up!" he bellowed.

I shut the fuck up that time.

He drove us deeper into South Sanford, out of South Ridge and closer to the club where we'd spent Thanksgiving. That part of town was called Southview. He pulled into a complex whose buildings looked brand new. The sign in front announced that they were the Medgar Evers apartments. There was a park and a pool in the middle of the circular complex. He stopped at a building with the letter G on it and parked next to a Furniture Revolution truck. Ken-Ken and PeeWee got out of it, carrying the stuff that I took with me when I got kicked out of my parents' house.

It was a three bedroom apartment on the top floor with brand new carpeting. He made a point of telling me that the elevator always worked. Some people in the lobby greeted him when we got on it.

"So this is the wife and the baby? You all make a lovely family," an old woman said to us. "Now this is a nice neighborhood. We tend to stand out from the rest of South Sanford in that way, and we're definitely not anything like South Ridge. Where are you all from again?"

Banger flexed his jaw instead of answering, so I told them, "Sapphire Cadre."

"Oh that's so good!" the woman said. "There's so many people trying to move here from Nat Turner and Frederick Douglass. The last thing we need are a bunch of South Ridge drug dealers and prostitutes taking over these buildings. Coming from Sapphire Cadre, I know you'll know how to conduct yourselves."

Banger stormed off the elevator and pulled me in the opposite direction of the way the woman walked. I was in love with the apartment as soon as we walked through the door. He already had big screen TVs and a big stereo in it. He told me to go to Furniture Revolution and pick out whatever I wanted later.

"You're not gonna come with me? I thought we were spending the day together?" I said.

"Nah. The shit I do ain't good enough for you, so I'm just gonna stop trying until the baby comes. Maybe he'll like me," he said in a dry, flat voice. "Gimme your car keys. I gotta put a new power steering pump in it before you hurt yourself trying to get around in that bucket." He took my car keys and dragged himself out the house, leaving me to feel like shit.

That car definitely broke our relationship. He made me drive it around just to prove a point, and he got distant. He never really left me alone for too long, but it felt like he wanted to be somewhere else when he was there. His boys were always at our house until stupid times of the night. Moosie tried to hang out with me, but who wanted to hang out with a woman who hit on you and thought it was funny? Squeak brought Shanae when he came, but I never got over her setting me up that day on the stoop. Plus, they always brought their bad ass kids. Those little demons knew they could tear up a house. Banger didn't care who he brought home as long as there was somebody there to keep him from having to be alone with me.

***

Furniture Revolution was filled with the most unique furniture I ever saw. The style could only be described as futuristic. They said everything in that store was made by hand by Chillz and his children. No wonder he got to stunt. I couldn't choose what I wanted. It would have helped to have Banger's input on something besides the leather living room set, but he seemed determined to stay mad about the car.

Chillz was sitting at a desk, talking on the phone, when I walked in. He looked up and smiled at me, urging me to come in and look around. I stopped to look at a king-sized bedroom set that looked like it was made for a god and goddess, but his conversation was more interesting.

"Yes, I will send you the money as soon as we get off this phone. I know she needs clothes for the changing seasons. She's running track this spring, too? Well, did she tell you what kind of sneakers she wants? When is her first track meet...? Because I want to come. Why else would I have asked...? Hope, we can't still be going through this shit. She's fifteen. I've been giving you money for years without a complaint. What's gonna happen if I show up...? You're gonna have me arrested for going to support my daughter at a track meet? Well, are you gonna be there? You work in the morning. Why wouldn't you be able to go in the evening? Well, what if I stay home, and the boys go? You can't treat them like you treat me. They called you 'Ma' at one point in time, too. They really want to see their sister. No, I don't want any problems. I just miss the hell out of my daughter and want to see her. Yeah. You'll get your money soon as I hang up the phone. Can I at least go buy the sneakers myself? No, you want the cash. Of course. I'll wire it to you when we hang up. Bye, Hope."

He slammed down the phone. His long face without the smile and with red-rimmed eyes made me sad for him.

He looked at me and said, "Promise me something? Whatever happens between you and Banger, don't keep his baby from him. He's gonna be a good father. Let him be that to that baby." He turned around a picture frame on his desk. That same girl that Selena and Rize went to see on Black Friday was in it. "This is my daughter. I haven't seen her in person since she was nine, and she only lives in East Sanford."

I looked at the picture. The girl was really dark and kind of had a big forehead. She had Chillz's smile but must have had her mother's everything else. "How did you get that picture of her?"

"She sent it through Rize. He goes to her sporting events, even though my family isn't supposed to have contact with her. She knows the truth about her mother. Kids always know. One day, I'll be able to be in her life again." He turned the picture back around. "Just don't do that to Banger. It hurts the baby the most."

I nodded my head.

The smile returned to his face, like he wasn't ready to cry his eyes out three seconds ago. He got up and showed me around the store.

"I hear you're pretty talented," he said as he showed me a dining room table. "Do you just design your clothes, or can you actually sew?"

"I can sew, crochet, and knit," I told him while I stopped to look at a pentagon shaped microwave cart.

He balled up his face. "Knit? Now why can't I picture busy body Monaysia sitting down in a rocking chair and knitting a sweater?"

I laughed. "I don't do it often, but sometimes when the mood hits me and I want a fly little scarf then I get busy."

"You ever think about opening up a store?" Chillz asked me.

"That's always been my goal," I admitted.

"Then me, Banger, and Selena will buy you a sewing machine and fabric, if you want. I know you're busy with school, but you can work on your stuff in your spare time. I've been hearing about that sketchbook for months. I'd like to see it, if it's something that you'd like to share. I know how some artists are about their shit." He stopped and watched me while I ran my hands along an oak table with a glass top. The diamond shape looked like it was about to take off for a dinner in space. I was in love with it.

"Sounds like you're trying to keep me busy," I said.

Even as just a sheepish grin, his smile was undefeated. I couldn't imagine growing up with a father who smiled like that. What was being disciplined by him like? They couldn't take him seriously while he fussed with those dimples popping the way they did.

"Maybe you'll have less time to make hasty decisions if your time is occupied doing something productive. I know you're bored, but, shorty, you're about to be a mother. I ain't saying life is about to stop, but you seem to want to live in the first twenty minutes of *New Jack*

*City* on a loop. That ain't how I raised my boys. I want them in, out, stacking money, and moving on to something that will put that money to good use for the community. This street is fifteen blocks long. There's no reason why there should only be three businesses on it." He stopped and studied me to make sure I understood what he was saying. "You could have your own department store on this street. People would come all the way across the bridge just to buy something that you made. But you're too busy focusing on being flashy for that to ever happen. You'll settle for a Rave when you could wait to get a Sak's."

"Chillz, I'm not as bad as y'all make me out to be," I defended myself. "I mean, y'all make me sound like some little gold digger."

Chillz gave me a side eye. "Didn't you set out to get pregnant by Banger?"

"He went in me raw," I protested.

"It's just me and you talking, Monaysia." His voice was soft. "I've already had this same discussion with him. I had to ask what made him go in someone raw on the first time. His answers were stupid." He dropped his voice an octave and broke into a lazy stance. "'Yo, Chillz. You see how fine she is. The pussy was too good to pull out.' Shit was just stupid as hell to me."

"He talks to you about that?" I asked incredulously.

"Yeah. Who the fuck else he gonna talk to? He told me you saw his moms before, and G-Ma don't do nothing but call him fast. He gotta talk to somebody about it," Chillz reasoned.

"I could never talk to my parents about sex that raw...no pun intended."

"Well, that's a problem, but that's a different conversation," Chillz said. "Talk to me, though. I heard you out there in the parking lot the day you told him you were pregnant. Why couldn't you just go to the movies with the nigga?"

"Banger didn't strike me as the type to have one main chick. He was nice to me the first night we went out, but then I didn't hear from him for weeks," I said.

"So you're the type who will do anything to get your way no matter what?" Chillz summed me up in one question. "If you picked up on that vibe, then why are y'all forcing a relationship where it don't fit? You're both miserable as hell together. This works out for you now, but what if the baby ain't his? Have you even heard from the other nigga?"

"I have, but I haven't responded, out of respect for my relationship," I lied.

Chillz seemed to see right through that. "So the baby's room at your crib has some shit in it from the other nigga?"

I shook my head. "He's waiting to see if the baby is his before he spends any time or money."

Chillz nodded. "Well, nobody can ever call you a dumb girl. You know who to get what you want from. I just wish you would put that type of energy into yourself. You get up every day to go to work at that job that I don't think you like. I could have a store and a warehouse set up for you across the street by next summer. I'd just need to know that I'm not gambling my money on your attitude.

"You could hook up with Peaches and do that shit together. I've been sending her all over the world every summer to learn different techniques and everything she needs to know. I hooked her up with this cat who owns luxury shopping malls all over the world, and he gave her a high saditty ass job as a garment technician for the major fashion houses. All she had to do was show me she wasn't gonna waste money doing it, and not just sit around whining about not having the flashiest cars and houses without a logical way to explain that she got the shit."

I glossed over him telling me that he was willing to fulfill my biggest fantasies to say, "Chillz, why do you act like there's something wrong with me wanting nice things? I told Banger on our first date that I wanted somebody to pay my bills and buy me gifts. We didn't even fuck on that date. He had weeks to sit on that, and he *still* went in me raw. So why am I the evil villain for laying down my expectations? He obviously comes from women who get what I want. Look at Selena. I've never seen tennis bracelets as sparkly as the ones she wears."

"First of all, Selena had some of that jewelry before we even got together. She used to model. You knew that, though, because you used to do the same thing," Chillz pointed out. "And Banger got you a $500 outfit the first night y'all spent together. He don't do shit like that."

Since my hips outgrew it, I'd forgotten all about the Iceberg outfit.

"I get it. Can he stand to do a little bit more for you than bitch about how much money shit costs? Yeah. That nigga even gets on *my* nerves with that shit. But you always talk about what you want, and I ain't heard nothing about you doing shit for him.

"You brought up Selena. Do you know what she does for me when I get home? She makes it somewhere I want to go at the end of the day. It ain't about no sexist bullshit, because Selena don't cook, and I had to hire a cleaning service to come in behind her ass. But my favorite part of the day is going home, not walking out the door. I know Banger can't say the same.

"Shouldn't a man who's been working three to four jobs, stacking for his family, want to look forward to going home to that family? Nah. He gotta worry about how much further Monaysia set them back. I ain't never met a man who was saving up to buy a car for his girl have to get right back to work buying parts for an eight-year-old bucket. Banger ain't perfect, but he ain't do shit to deserve the way you be giving him your ass to kiss."

So after my lecture, I was back on the track we started down before Mommy gave me that insurance check. To boot, I had a beautifully furnished apartment with pieces I'd never seen in anybody's house in Sapphire Cadre. I was always taking pictures in different rooms in the house, getting them developed in an hour, and dropping them off at Mommy's house so that she could brag to all of her friends. She was so happy to be able to send out the Memorial Day cards I made using pictures I took in my living room, showing how beautifully pregnancy treated me.

With my next paycheck, I took Banger to dinner and the movies. I also bought him a gift. He didn't wear jewelry, and Mommy told me to never buy a man sneakers, so I made him the jacket that was on the sketchpad he looked at in the staircase in Nat Turner. He was surprised by the gesture and loved the jacket. He wore it all over and came home every day to tell me about people saying they wanted one. It seemed like the gloom that was over us when I bought that hoopty was lifted.

After seeing how serious about making clothes I was, Chillz, Selena, and Banger brought a sewing machine home. It was top of the line, even better than anything I had at school in New York. Peaches had a surplus of fine fabrics and yarn with silk threads. I put them all in that third bedroom and set up a little studio. Banger bought me whatever I said I needed for it.

When I asked him why buying all that stuff wouldn't bring unneeded attention, he looked at me like I had five heads.

"This is the right kind of attention. You doing shit that explains why we're able to buy the shit that we got in our crib now. The more you do, the more I can buy for you. Now hurry up and get those baby clothes finished. Lynn cleared out a spot in the shop that you can sell them out of," he told me.

"Why would she do that? She doesn't even like me," he said.

"You gotta like people to get money with them?" he asked. "She got her own goals for that spa. If you and Peaches can get together and start making clothes to sell out of it, then that gets her one step closer to her goals."

At that point, I hoped to God that baby was his, because I didn't want that life to end. Somehow, it was even better than the one I had planned when I started with this dumb ass idea. Suddenly, my dumb ass idea wasn't a dumb ass idea anymore.

The first Saturday in June, Kidra called me a million times to remind me not to be late for the baby shower. Banger bought me a new outfit and sent me to get my weave tightened and my nails done, but he refused to come to the party. He said that wasn't a man thing, but he would pick me up in a truck big enough to bring the gifts home.

Selena was the one who took me. She, Shanae, Melinda, Big Grams, and Chillz's sisters were the ones who came from Banger's family. I knew those messy ass sisters only came to see if my daddy would show up. Luckily, he felt the same way about baby showers that Banger did. I didn't really want Shanae's ass there, but it looked good to have people from Banger's family there. G-Ma couldn't get away from the kids, so she sent food. When she found out G-Ma was sending food, Big Grams cooked twice as much. They seemed like they were in the same type of competition as my mother was with her sister.

Speaking of that cow, she and Chrissy stood at the curb outside of the picket fence. Aunt Marvine declared to everyone who passed that she didn't support going to a baby shower before a bridal shower. That was funny, because Mommy said that Aunt Marvine never had either. She claimed that Aunt Marvine just showed up with Chrissy one day and wouldn't answer any questions. They had all the questions for me, though, about the car Banger dropped me off in, where he worked, and where we lived. I answered none and just left Chrissy staring after the Suburban after Banger kissed me and drove away.

I was surprised that Banger's family brought gifts to the shower after everything they already did for me, but their cars were loaded. They said they were from extended members of Banger's family who couldn't come. Mommy peeked at tags and read the name Joy Gilead.

"I heard that woman's running for the mayor of East Sanford. How's she related to your baby, Monaysia?" Mommy asked.

I looked to Lynn, who said, "That's my sister."

Mommy looked at another name and exclaimed, "How the hell do you know who Bobby Jackson is?"

I stared at her with my face wrinkled and was surprised when Banger's aunts did too.

"He owns most of the land here in Sapphire Cadre. He built this neighborhood. Why wouldn't she know him?" Renee asked.

I watched Mommy fidget without answering.

"Marliss Brantley? My mama used to listen to her albums. We used to eat at her buffet all the time. Monaysia, exactly who the hell is this boyfriend of yours?"

Selena and the sisters cracked up at Mommy's question.

Melinda sat in the corner and fidgeted the whole time. She was so quiet that we forgot she was there. It was weird seeing her in jeans instead of a miniskirt. She looked like she couldn't function without her legs showing.

My family and friends bought me a lot of clothes and diapers. Since I told Mommy about the cradle, crib, and bassinet Chillz built me by hand, she and Kidra bought a Mickey Mouse playpen and toys. They even got me a baby Mickey Mouse cake.

It was a really cute day until Siraya and Yvette came in all late. At least Siraya apologized for having to stay at work until her relief came. Yvette had the nerve to be empty handed, but went straight for the food. Both of their eyes roamed around the room. Disappointment put frowns on both of their faces.

"Your baby daddy's friends ain't get here yet?" Yvette asked.

"That's why y'all came here? You thought you was gonna get a date at my baby shower?"

"No, girl. We came to tell you that Yolanda said she's gonna stomp you out after that baby is born."

Selena looked up at Yvette when she said that but kept her mouth closed.

Lynn, who never missed an opportunity to give an opinion, said, "What kinds of friends you got that bring this type of drama to your house? A real friend wouldn't let nobody say nothing like that about you, especially while you're pregnant. A real friend would've taken care of it without you ever knowing about it until you're old, sitting down, drinking wine, and reminiscing over whatever happened to old so-and-so."

"That just makes me look at you like you suspect," Renee piped up, looking directly at Yvette when she spoke. "What did you do when the girl said that?"

Yvette stared at them like they had her trapped.

I was surprised that they had anything to say in my defense. That pumped me up.

"You tell Yolanda I said she knows exactly where the fuck I'm at, and that that she ain't gotta wait until my baby drops. That bitch can't fight. I'll beat her ass while I'm pregnant for what she did to my car."

I truly felt like Banger and I could have been much happier had Yolanda not crashed my car.

Yvette and Siraya stayed around anyway, waiting for Banger to show up after the shower. Of course, Rize was with him. Rico and

Trigga came along just in case extra hands were needed. Yvette and Siraya strutted around, batting their eyelashes like some horny hens. Rico and Trigga looked right past them, but Rize went to Siraya and asked her name. Even though she was puzzled about him not remembering her, she gave him her phone number again. We went on a double date that night. He fucked her and didn't call her the next day. Yvette was mad that she stayed at my baby shower that long but didn't get any play. I had to get new friends.

***

Just because he felt that baby showers were women only events didn't mean my dad was going to be left out of giving gifts. When I finally called him, he insisted on having me come to his new house for dinner. It was a cute little single family house in Eastview. I resisted the urge to ask if he was paying two mortgages.

He never did indoor housework when he and Mommy were together, so it was cute to see him running around, straightening things. I got a kick out of the thought of him doing all the dusting and dish washing that he made Kidra and me do as kids.

"You're so much cuter than your mom was when she carried you and Kidra. I bet she's jealous. Do you know what you're having yet?"

"A boy."

I never saw my dad jump higher or heard him scream louder than when I told him he was about to have a grandson. The smile on his face never left after I gave him the news. He reached out and grabbed my belly with both of his hands, though there wasn't much to grab.

"A grandson! I'm having a grandson!" He pulled me against him and hugged me. "I'm gonna buy him a basketball tomorrow!"

The front door opened. I thought maybe Dad had a roommate, but he tensed and started picking at his cuticles.

"Were you expecting somebody?" I asked.

"There's somebody I wanted you to meet. I, uh, don't know how to introduce you, though. She's completely different from your mother," was his answer.

My lip curled. "She's supposed to be. You're supposed to upgrade after a breakup. Of course, *I'm* not gonna think anybody is better than my own mama, but whatever. I ain't gonna stress your little girlfriend out."

He looked at me for a few minutes with his lips twisted and picked his cuticles some more. His eyes went to the door, and mine followed. My mouth dropped open. Melinda's eyes met mine, and then she quickly looked away.

"Please tell me you're fuckin her mama, and this is just a meet and greet for the whole family," I said.

Dad looked from Melinda to me. "You know her?"

"She was in my sociology class last semester. We just had lunch together last week. We hang out often. We're, like, friends or something." I folded my arms and stared at Melinda.

"I didn't know this was your daddy when I started talking to him, Nay," she quickly said. "I didn't expect it to get this serious. I'm sorry I didn't say anything."

At least her being all motherly and shit to me finally made sense. I shook my head at the both of them.

"Whatever. This ain't my business. You're grown. Dad's grown and soon to be unmarried. It's all good."

Dad gritted his teeth. "Just like that? You're not gonna flip on me later, are you?"

I sank into the couch. Suddenly, I could feel that it was softer than most couches, upholstered with a premium fabric. The wooden frame smelled freshly chopped. I looked around and realized that it was the furniture that made his house so cute. He'd gotten it all from Furniture Revolution. It took several breaths to keep me calm.

"Flip for what?" I asked. "I have a baby to worry about. I'm not thinking about y'all. I wish that Melinda would have told me about this *before I invited her into my mother's house,* but other than that? This ain't my business. Do you have any apple juice, Dad?"

Melinda held up a bag that I didn't notice her carrying. "I ran out to the store to get you some when Eddie told me you were coming over."

We ate in an uncomfortable silence. I wanted my dad to stop shooting me looks every few seconds. Of course I had questions, but I already had the answers. My dad was "Edwin that be in the bar on 110th and Hyman,"and Melinda wasn't the high profile escort I thought she was. She was nothing but a hooker who settled for niggas who used coupons. She was nobody for me to look up to.

I was on fire when I walked through the door that night. My attitude must have gotten into the house before me, because Banger and Rize both groaned when they heard the door close. They were putting together the swing that I got from my baby shower and arguing about it missing a screw. I stood right over them, not caring that they were patting the floor for the tiny piece.

"Did you know about my dad and Melinda?" I demanded.

They both slowly turned their heads toward me. A nervous laugh was leaking from Rize's mouth. Banger didn't answer me.

"Have y'all been laughing at me behind my back this whole time?" I asked.

"Of course not. I feel sorry for you. Your parents try to hide all their dirt behind bragging about you, and they're mad they can't do it anymore. Fuck them niggas." Banger rolled over and screwed two parts of the swing together.

"But you're not answering my question. Did you know about my dad and Melinda?" I pressed.

"Quit asking me questions in the crib. What difference is the answer gonna make?" he asked.

Rize nudged Banger. "She looks hurt."

"Some parents ain't shit. They'll call you names for doing the shit that they do better than they do it. Fuck 'em." He shrugged.

In the middle of the summer, I stood in Public Speaking and got ready to argue against the death penalty. That class was the last place that I wanted to be, but I stuck to that conversation I had with Chillz and kept myself busy. I took two courses for each summer session of school. My doctor took me out of work at the end of June, so when I wasn't in class, I was either at home, working on designs and patterns, knitting baby clothes, or somewhere eating with Melinda. Every now and again, I went down to Nat Turner to practice mothering with Shanae's babies or the babies at G-Ma's house.

While I was supposed to be defending my stance on the death penalty, I thought about my plans for that night. Banger was taking me out to dinner with Peaches so that we could plan a kids' clothing collection. She was still learning how to make patterns and sew, but she was way more educated on how fabrics sold than me. Then, we were going to pack my overnight bag for the hospital. I still had two weeks before the baby was due. I didn't really give a damn about the death penalty.

As soon as I got my first word out, it felt like I peed on myself. There was a big gush on the floor. Everyone heard it and groaned out their disgust.

"Did it get on my podium?" my teacher joked while he walked to me to help me get around the mess. "Who do I need to call?"

I had him page Banger and put in my due date. Then, I just sat there and waited. I was going to drive myself to the hospital, but the student health center advised me against it. The student health nurse called my doctor, and then I told them to call Selena.

Selena peered at me when campus security escorted her into the classroom with the campus nurse and said, "You're very calm. Shouldn't you be screaming from contractions or something?"

"I don't feel any. Is that weird? Should we call Shanae to see if this is normal?" I suggested.

"Girl, get in the car," she said. "Chillz wants to know where your bag is."

"Um..."

She rolled her eyes. "Of course you didn't pack it yet. Who am I talking to? I'll just buy you new shit."

"Are you feeling any contractions at all?" the nurse asked me.

I shook my head. She walked me down to the student health office while campus security made a way for Selena to get her car to the front door.

I asked the nurse if I could use her phone and dialed Best's number to tell him what happened.

"Aw shit. Look at you about to pull it off," he said cheerfully.

I recoiled at the reaction. "Aren't you coming to the hospital?"

"Ain't the other nigga gonna be there?" he asked me.

"Yeah, but—"

"So what am I supposed to do, stand on one side of the room and take turns telling you to push? You tryna get me murked?"

"No, but Best—"

"Just have that nigga get tested while he's there. He's more likely the daddy than me, since you never let me raw dog you. Other than that, just call me if his results come back negative. Then, I'll be around."

"Best, I can't believe you're leaving me out here like this a second time," I said.

"I hear you're well taken care of. Just let me know if it ain't his. Then, I'll be around."

Security took me out to Selena's car and had us sign a release saying that we didn't want an ambulance. Rize or somebody else went to get my car after being informed several times that they would tow my vehicle if it was left there overnight.

"I haven't called my parents and my sister!" I panicked when we pulled up to the maternity entrance at the hospital.

Banger was right at the door with a wheelchair and a smile. G-Ma stood off to the side, praying. Chillz and Rize sat on either side of her with their heads bowed and eyes closed. The rest of the family quickly arrived with more baby gifts and even stuff for me. I hoped to God that baby was Banger's.

"You feel okay? You don't seem like you're in pain," Banger asked me as we were forced to sit at the desk and fill out forms that we were supposed to complete and mail back a month ago.

"I'm good. Just give this lady $200 so that I can get in a room. My dress is wet."

He handed the woman sitting behind the desk the money. A nurse came and pushed me up to a room with ducks on the wall and told me to get into the bed so that she could give me an IV. The moment I stood, I felt like I was getting ripped in half from between my legs. Instinct told me grabbing the bed rail would take away some of the pain. I didn't want to scream. I thought Banger would laugh if I did, but he dropped down right next to me and rubbed my back.

"Was that your first contraction?" the nurse asked me.

"I don't know what the fuck that was, but give me some drugs so that I don't feel it again!" I hollered. "Why can't I close my legs? What is this in between my legs?"

The nurse ordered me to get into the bed. Banger gently rolled me into it. She looked up my dress and said, "The baby's crowning."

She called for the doctor. Instead of my doctor, someone called a hospitalist entered the room. He told me to push. I didn't want to do it without drugs. He yelled that on my next contraction I had to push. As I did, I decided that I was never having another child again in life. I didn't care how much money the daddy had. I never wanted to feel that shit again.

I was still in pain, but the doctor announced that it was a boy and then told me to push some more.

"Why? I'm having twins?" I screamed.

Banger's head jerked up so fast that I wanted to laugh, but I was in too much pain. The doctor told me that I had to push out the afterbirth. Fuck afterbirth. I swore I was never getting pregnant again. My doctor came in all late and put that bloody ass baby on my dress, making sure that I could never wear it again. I tried to catch a peek at him to see who he looked like, but they took him away once he started screaming in my ear.

"Do you want to do the mouth swabs and blood tests now or later?" my doctor asked me.

Banger looked like he wanted to say something, but he just stood there while they took the mouth and blood samples from all of us. Then, he watched over the nurses and doctors while they did their thing with the baby. When they were done measuring and cleaning him, Banger held his arms out first. He sat down with him and started telling him how much he loved him. I just kept praying that it was his baby.

After making me go to the bathroom, they took the baby and me to an even bigger room. That's where I got to hold and get a good look at him. He didn't look like anybody. He was pale with a fat face, and his eyes were two slits that didn't open. He yawned. It was the cutest thing I'd ever seen in my life.

"What are we gonna name him?" Banger asked, watching me hold him with a smile on his face. That smile was messing with my head. It was the sunniest thing I'd ever seen.

"I'm gonna wait until tomorrow. The doctor said the test results will be back by then," I said.

He shrugged. "I think we should name him now, but I'll do it your way." He came and took the baby from me.

A big, burly nurse appeared in the doorway and barked out the strangest command:

"Go ahead and let him suckle! Ten minutes on each breast!" Her voice was like a bullhorn.

"Oh no. Don't y'all got some formula? I'm not about to have my knockers sagging."

"You need to at least try," the nurse insisted.

"You gonna pay for me to get my knockers lifted?" I challenged her through bucked eyes. When she scowled instead of answering, I said, "Aight then. Bring me some formula."

Banger shot me a look but didn't say anything. He took the formula the nurse brought him and went right back to doting on the baby. He took off the baby's hat and showed me a head full of hair. I couldn't wait to send him to Lynn to get it braided.

"His eyes are the same color as yours," Banger commented in a soft, soothing voice.

I jolted around in the bed. "They are? He opened them? Let me see!"

"Nope. He's only opening his eyes for his daddy." He pressed his nose against the baby's. When he pulled his face away, the baby sneezed. That made him smile even harder. "Can we please name him now?"

"What if—"

He shook his head. "This is my baby. I can feel it. I know what I did that night. Four times, if I remember correctly."

"Banger, I let another nigga hit within 16 hours of you. Let's just wait. I just...I just don't want you to get caught up in something you don't have to."

He sighed. In a quiet voice he asked, "So you want me to leave until the results come back?"

My heart dropped. I didn't really want to be alone.

"Yeah... I'll hit you on the hip when they discharge me." I reached out for the baby.

Banger made a buzzer noise. "You're wrong! I'm staying here with my baby. Get the fuck on with that bullshit."

I prayed that I wouldn't be homeless soon.

Soon after that, the room was filled with his family and mine. Both of my parents came and stood on opposite sides of the room. Daddy had the nerve to bring Melinda with him. That just made the situation sticky, because I didn't know if she called Best to come up there or not. She gave me a half smile. I just wanted to know if she had my blunt and my gin and juice. She patted her purse, and I gave her a huge smile.

I introduced my parents to G-Ma, Chillz, and Selena. Mommy was so busy being a hostess at the baby shower that she didn't really remember any of the guests. Daddy stared at Selena for a little too long. Melinda caught it but kept quiet. If Selena noticed, she didn't say anything. Everybody talked about which of Banger's features the baby had, like I didn't have anything to do with the baby's existence.

This man that Banger swore I met on Thanksgiving came in with Nyir. They both carried flowers, balloons, and all kinds of gifts. He bent over and kissed me on my forehead before he introduced himself as "Unc". He was Chillz's best friend and Banger's other father figure. He looked important, wearing a sweater vest and khakis while typing into a Palm Pilot. He answered a call but told whoever was on the phone to call him back when they had his money and then flashed his toothpaste commercial smile at everyone in the room. His presence was so large that he even made Chillz look small. If Chillz was their god, then Unc was their god's supervisor. I couldn't believe the number of gifts, flowers, and balloons he brought with him. I was tired, but I wanted to open them all right then. I knew a man that powerful looking had connections to the finest gifts.

A hush went over the room. Unc bent over and looked in the baby's face. He inspected his fingers, ran his hand over the baby's head, and then stopped at his ears and chuckled. "Oh yeah. That's your baby, son. He got them little pointy elf ears you had when you was a baby."

G-Ma, Big Grams, and a woman named Sheila looked at the baby and agreed.

Mommy cleared her throat. "Why did you make that comment?"

Lisa nudged Unc in his ribs.

"Oh, that's just something we say in South Ridge," Unc quickly said.

Mommy was too busy lusting after him to ask any more questions. I had to admit, that brown man was fine, but then I saw similarities between him and Banger. My baby daddy could be that in a couple of years if he kept working as hard as people said he did. Maybe Mommy and I could go on double dates with them once I got out of the hospital. He was a definite upgrade from my dad.

There was a commotion outside of the room. We all turned our heads to the door. Banger's eyes got big, and then he dropped his head when he recognized the voices. His mother burst into the room while Marcus tried to pull her back.

"Nay-Nay, you know these people?" Mommy asked.

"It's fine, Mommy," I stammered, unsure of how big of a lie I was telling.

"I can't believe no one called me to tell me my grandbaby was born!" Banger's mom burst into the room and roared. Her hair and body were even thinner than before.

"Darlene, please don't embarrass your son in front of his girlfriend's people!" G-Ma yelled.

Banger's mom turned to G-Ma. "You the main one turned him against me, and I'm supposed to be your daughter. You and them two over there." She pointed to Lynn and Selena, who were standing in a line, waiting to hold the baby.

G-Ma wrinkled her nose and shook her head. "Long as you got that monkey on your back, you ain't no daughter of mine. I'll pray for you, but you gotta leave. Marcus, you wanna come see your nephew, or you gotta chase behind your mama?"

Marcus looked like he really wanted to stay. "I'm gonna see if I can get her checked in here, and then I'll be back."

"I ain't going!" Darlene shrieked.

Unc hopped up, and the woman named Sheila followed him. She took Darlene by her arm and dared her to fight back.

"Stay here, Marcus. We'll take care of your mama, and you'll come home with us," Unc said. He turned back to me. "Congratulations. Beautiful baby. Nice to meet you, parents." He winked at my mother.

My dad was steaming, but Mommy blushed and looked like I did when I knew I was setting up a date later.

When the hospital announced that visiting hours were over, everybody but Banger left. He still had the baby and told me to get some rest. I told him he was the one who needed to be resting since he worked so much.

"You just pushed a baby out of you in four minutes. Just get some rest. You're a mother now. You need it."

I fell asleep, but not for long. A nurse came in and said that she had to take the baby to the nursery to run some tests.

"I hope your mother gets better," I said after the nurse left, just to have something to say.

"She won't," he snapped. "And don't ever let her come around our baby."

Him saying 'our baby' still wasn't sitting right with me.

Seconds passed, and I asked, "How come Marcus doesn't live with G-Ma?"

"Because he gotta take care of our mother. The only reason she had on clean clothes was because he made her put them on. He thinks she's gonna come home and be a mother again. I don't know why. She left us when he was a baby."

"I'm sorry. I didn't even mean to make you talk about her. I know you don't like to."

"It's all good. I gotta make sure I can answer these questions if my son ever asks me."

I fought sleep while he was feeling chatty. "Whatever happens with the tests tomorrow, thank you so much for the way you've taken care of me. I'm sorry I've been ungrateful and difficult. You don't deserve any of the B.S. I've given you."

He looked surprised to hear me say those things. He had no response. I went to sleep, trembling at the thought of being homeless after leaving the hospital.

My doctor came in the next morning, laughing about my ten minutes of labor. We thought he'd bring the DNA test results, but he told us they would take weeks to get back. That made my heart sink. I waited for Banger to get up and leave, but he stayed right there while the doctor told us how perfect our baby was.

"So what are we gonna name him?" Banger asked me when the doctor left.

I sighed. He groaned at me mockingly. Before something about waiting could come out my mouth, he hit the call bell and asked when the people would come to fill out the birth certificate.

"Hurry up and decide on a name before they get here," he urged me.

With one last deep sigh, I pointed to the table across the room where my purse sat and told him to bring it to me. The piece of paper I'd written baby names on sat in the bottom of it. I took it out, unfolded it, and handed it to him to read. When the woman from the office of vital statistics came, we put NyQuest Wise Bailey on our son's birth certificate.

After she left, Banger finally allowed himself to fall asleep. I lay in bed holding the baby, trying to get him to open his eyes for me. He seemed to only want to sleep until he was in Banger's arms. Then he was wide awake, waiting to see what his daddy would say to him next. I was a little bit jealous of their bond.

Instead of worrying about who his father was, I was able to appreciate how beautiful the baby who lay in my arms was. I was a little worried that my sporadic weed smoking while pregnant would give him a birth defect, but he was perfect. He was 7 pounds, 2 ounces, and 23 inches long. Unc was right. His ears were a little pointy at the top. Banger's kind of were too. I laughed at the part of him I hadn't noticed before. There was nothing else distinctive about him yet. I couldn't go to sleep. It was hard to believe that I carried something that cute inside of me.

Rize came into the room and asked for his nephew. I looked at the clock. It was 9am on the dot, the exact minute of the beginning of visiting hours. He brought breakfast food for us from Peter's Kitchen, the restaurant that was next to Hair Revolution. That place made the best bacon I ever tasted.

"Can you come sit with me?" I whispered. "I need to talk to you about something important."

He pulled a chair next to the bed and then took the baby while I stuffed my face with that bacon. "So you got my brother as a baby-daddy, just like you wanted. Congratulations. You hooked a good one."

"We haven't even gotten the results back yet," I pointed out.

"He beeped me and put a bunch of ones on the screen, meaning he knows it's his baby," Rize replied.

"What was the code if he felt like he wasn't?" I wondered.

"403," Rize answered.

"Why those three numbers?" I asked.

"It spells out 'hoe' if you turn it upside down."

That remark made me find out how much it hurt to laugh after having a baby. It shouldn't have been that funny to me. In a few weeks, he could be putting the numbers 403 into Rize's pager and putting me out of the house.

"I need you to help me," I whispered.

He stopped looking at the baby and turned his attention to me. "With what?"

"Being what your friend deserves," I told him. "He's been better to me than even my own family has been, no matter how stupid I've been. I didn't appreciate that until now. What if he isn't the father? I could be out on the curb with a baby.

"Before I felt like — you know — oh well. I kept it real with him, and he still chose to take care of me. But now, looking at the baby has him feeling a whole different way."

"First of all, you and me both know that you won't be on the curb with no baby," Rize said. "His name is on the certificate. He just took the test to stop any questions from popping up later."

"You don't think he'll get it removed if the test results come back saying he's not the father?" I asked incredulously.

The scowl on his face told me he hated that the answer was no.

"So what you want me to do?"

"Be on my side, please?" I begged him. "I don't know how to be a girlfriend good enough for him. I never had to think about nobody but myself, because the niggas I fucked with were only worried about themselves. I don't know what makes him happy, but I wanna do whatever it is."

Rize sat back with the baby, scrunched his mouth, and nodded.

"Well, first off, you gotta stop that friend shit. That nigga right there is my brother. I'm closer to him than I am my blood brothers. That's saying a lot, because you see how close I am to them. You gotta understand, though, that I will kill for that nigga Shaan. It's been nights that I wanted to strangle you for being ungrateful, but y'all business ain't my business. Just know if you do anything to hurt him, I'm gonna get somebody to fuck you up."

Rize rocked NyQuest to remind himself where he was. That was when I saw how deep his hate for me went.

"Keep it real, I don't even understand why he fucked with your ass after he saw what you did to your friend, nahmean? I see it in you. You wanna change right now, but that snake is always gonna live in you. I don't know what you want from me, but I don't trust you."

I sighed. I'd never met a more difficult man to crack. Usually, men wanted sex from me and would do whatever I asked to get it. Rize didn't even seem like he was attracted to me. He almost seemed to hate the fact that I existed.

"I'm not interested in gaining your trust. All I'm trying to do is build a family with your brother."

"So talk to him about it. You don't need me for that," he said. "You need to talk to him about what you want."

"That nigga don't talk, and you and me both know that," I protested. "Before the baby was born, he just seemed to come home and hate being there. I want him to be happy with our family."

"Then stop being stupid," Rize told me. "In my eyes, you're way too childish to have a baby, and you're too selfish. If you were a little bit more mature, you could already see that he's happy as fuck to be with you when you ain't stressing him out. You gotta listen to that nigga when he tells you about money, too. If that nigga don't know nothing else, he knows about his dough. You can't be fuckin up cuz you wanna be flashy. I'll never forget how you was looking in them niggas' faces in the club on Thanksgiving. My boy deserves better than your spotlight desiring ass."

I sighed. "Rize, I'm sorry I treated him that way."

"Yeah, you are right now, because the other nigga who was supposed to be there for you ain't here. But wait until the next time a nigga with deep pockets starts paying you attention. You better get smarter, because it don't get no better than my brother."

For three days, I stayed in the hospital, watching Banger and NyQuest form a bond. I wondered if my own father was that in love with me when I was born. I wished I was as excited about being a mother, but I was jealous and fearful. I had no backup plan. Mommy was at peace now, but she wasn't letting me back in the house with a baby I conceived without knowing who the father was.

We slept while they took the baby away for the hundreds of tests they had to perform. Banger climbed into the bed with me, kissing me and thanking me. The news was on the TV. We didn't really pay attention to it until a kidnapping story made Banger perk up.

*"...As the body of a fourth kidnapping victim is found in the south end of the Benjamin Banneker Forest, citizens question the parallels between the kidnappings in the 1980s with this most recent rash. With Jeremiah Revolution set to be executed in just three months for the 1980s kidnappings, questions arise over whether or not he has descendants working for him."*

Banger's grip tightened around me as Hope Thomas continued to talk. He kept muttering that she was a lying, conniving bitch. I was taken back to the day that Selena made me turn off the news and wondered if they'd discussed it. Banger never brought it up if they did. He cut his eyes at me as though he could read my thoughts. Then, he muted the TV and got this real serious look on his face. I didn't have a choice to do anything except give him my attention.

"One time, you said you wanted to make clothes for that slut on the TV. Why?" he questioned me.

"Look at her. The bitch is bad, and she always got something fly on. If I can get her to wear one of my gowns when she gets one of the awards that she gets every year, everybody will be wanting to wear my clothes," I said.

"So it's just about the way she looks?" he wondered.

"That's most of it, but she always came to the career fairs when I was in school and talked about what it was like to be her. I always wanted to spend days of my life telling little girls what it was like to be me. That's how you know you lived a dope life," I told him. "All the boys in school used to be all over her. They weren't like that in your school?"

"We ain't have no damn career fairs in my school," he grumbled.

"How? They used to give us the whole week off to go to them," I told him. "All types of people would be there."

"We ain't get that in South Sanford," he repeated.

"Not even on Fridays?" I asked him.

"When we went to learn trades? Oh. Yeah. We went to that bullshit then, but we ain't never get called back to shadow nobody," he said.

"For real?" I asked.

"You getting off the subject. What do you think about the shit she reports about?" he asked me.

When I gave him a blank look, he turned the volume back on.

*"...Channel 3 was the first station to break the story of Jeremiah Revolution's relation to the kidnappings in the 1980s. His son, William Revolution, was also arrested and served time for those charges until he was released after winning an appeal. As more bodies turn up, all eyes turn to him and his family to see how closely connected they are to the disappearance of the children."*

I continued with the blank look until a mugshot was plastered on the TV screen.

"That looks like Chillz, but younger," I remarked.

"That *is* Chillz when he was younger," Banger informed me.

I snapped my head so that I was looking at him. "Chillz is Jeremiah Revolution's son? Nigga, what the fuck do you got me caught up in? Jeremiah Revolution is a serial killer and a child molester."

Banger grabbed me by both of my shoulders and stared into my eyes so hard that I thought he was going to burn a hole through my face.

"Watch your muthafuckin mouth when you're talking about him. That man was the closest thing I had to a grandfather. I'm trying to be calm and understanding, because I know you don't know what really goes on, but this is the only time I'm gonna be able to say this to you without popping off," he told me.

I struggled to get him to loosen his grip on my shoulders. He apologized and then cupped my face with his hands. His voice was whisper-quiet when he spoke.

"Whatever that bitch on that TV screen says is a lie. Her whole career and all the awards she got are based off of lies that she gets paid to tell. She's the reason why my grandfather has been in jail since the '80s and will probably die there before the end of the year. He didn't do none of the shit she said he did. She got audio of him saying something about building a health center and took it to the police. They were targeting him and the rest of my family for feeding people in South Ridge and used it to take him down."

"Banger, that sounds like some Black Panther shit," I commented.

"That's pretty much what he was, except he was for the poor Black people who got left behind when Sanford County was on the come-up," Banger informed me. "You don't have no reason to believe nothing I'm saying, but you could ask G-Ma for the full story."

"Is that why you don't like to talk inside buildings and cars?" I wondered aloud.

He nodded. "Seen too many niggas' words twisted and turned into the police to get locked up or killed."

"Oh," I said.

"I'm gonna tell you something else. That bitch on the TV that you wanna be so bad is a snake. The shit is personal with us, but she don't give a fuck who she bulldozes over to get what she wants. Chillz said he saw a lot of her in you the first time you came around, and I want you to prove everybody wrong," Banger said.

I hung my head in shame.

"Nay, listen to me. You don't owe nobody shit in this world, but I just want you to promise me one thing to make up for all the bullshit that you took me through since I met you. Please?" he begged.

His pupils were jumping, and his grip on my face was getting tight. I pushed his hands away from my face and locked my fingers with him.

"I'm listening," I told him.

"Keep you and our son away from that bitch and anybody who associates with her. I know you got dreams of her walking into your store and buying everything off the racks, but it's a different way for you to blow up, a better way. I promise that whatever she promises you ain't worth it. You're the baddest chick in The County. She can use you to do whatever she wants and then pay you to be quiet about it. Just stay away from her ass. Stay away from her, and keep my son away from anybody she's ever around. If you get invitations to police balls, don't go. The mayor of East Sanford wants you to dress him, say no. I know that's fucking up your paper, but all money ain't good money. The shit that crew is handing out comes with a price, and the price is either your life or your freedom."

"But why are they saying that your grandfather and Chillz did that shit, Banger? Do you know what kind of horror stories they tell us about them in the county's history?" I asked him.

He nodded his head. "The worst part about that is that in a little less than a year, unless a miracle happens, he'll die with those lies on his name."

Tears were in his eyes. I reached out, ready to wipe them, but he denied their presence.

"So how am I supposed to know who's down with her clique?" I asked.

"Anybody she has anything good to say anything about," he answered. "It's mostly her and the chief of police, but he got kids. If you're ever around a nigga named Andrew Jones, get the fuck out of dodge. Him and his sister, Loretta. Other than that, not too many people fuck with her. She burns her bridges real quick."

I sighed away my disappointment about my childhood hero and rested my head against him.

"I can't see Chillz doing anything like that to kids," I said. "I promise whoever you don't want me around, I won't have myself or our son around."

He stroked my head. It was the most tender he'd ever been with me.

"I got a question to ask you. Growing up, what did they tell you about the kidnappings?" he wondered.

"That people kept having kids they couldn't afford, so they killed them or sold them for drugs, because everybody in South Sanford is a crackhead," I explained, and tried to adjust the way I was laying as a pain struck through the middle of my body.

Banger got up and got an ice pad. He helped me change my panties and the bloody pad under me without cringing or commenting while he continued the conversation. "And who the fuck bought the kids?"

I shrugged. "I never thought to ask that question. I was just told to stay out of South Ridge because kids disappear from over there."

"Did anybody ever disappear from over there where you stay at?" he wondered.

I scrunched my face. "One or two boys, but their families just put up missing children posters and then moved away after nobody helped them find them."

It was his turn to scrunch his face. "Why the fuck would you move away from your home if your child went missing?" he asked. "What if the child comes home and finds a different family living there?"

"I think something happened to the families, but I don't know. That's something our parents only talked about at parties when they got drunk, and we were supposed to be asleep but were sneaking wine coolers into our rooms. Whatever I tell you about that is gonna be a lie that Arbor Mist told me about what I heard." I tried to laugh, but he didn't join me.

A blue-eyed man in a navy blue suit came onto the TV screen. He looked white at first glance, but the waves in his dark hair told me at least one of his parents was Black. Banger's whole face pulled tight as he watched the man take a seat next to Hope. She greeted the chief of police named Tennessee Jones and asked him what his department's plan was for the missing children.

"It's up to all of the citizens to help us. We can't be everywhere all the time," he said with a snide smile on his face.

Hope Thomas' smile was just as diabolical, and I wondered why I hadn't noticed it before.

"Are you sure? A superhero like you?"

The two of them laughed in a way that made my skin crawl. I'd seen the two of them on my TV dozens of times, acting that exact same way, but it never bothered me until that day. Another of my lifelong goals faded, and I started to question if the things I spent my whole childhood working for would ever pay off. Now here I was, on the brink of being a single mother, stuck in Sanford County to raise a baby who was part of a family with a bullseye on it. I closed my eyes to squeeze away tears. Crying wasn't something that I did a lot of, but I'd backed myself into a stupid corner. I was even further from the possibility of getting to Paris where all of my other goals could grow toward being accomplished. Banger tried to resume our conversation, but the realization that I'd messed up my life as well as a baby who didn't ask to be a part of my bullshit made me want to go to sleep forever.

The weeks the hospital said would take for the paternity results to reach us turned into a month and a half. Things were awkward when I went to my postpartum checkup and still didn't have a confirmation. Banger was there with me, so proudly holding the baby while I talked to the doctor about how I felt since giving birth. When my doctor congratulated Banger on getting confirmation that he was NyQuest's father, neither of us mentioned that we hadn't received the results yet. Instead, Banger asked what he could do to make motherhood as comfortable for me as possible. He said that he didn't think I was ready to go back to work yet, citing that I slept a lot and didn't have much of an appetite.

What Banger didn't know was that I was terrified that he was going to put me out of the apartment if that baby wasn't his. Every day, I checked my bank account. Because I didn't have to pay bills during my pregnancy, I had more than enough in my savings account to live on my own. I just wouldn't be able to afford anything else. I'd be a regular, working class person with a regular job at the phone company. That made me feel like I was living in a blackhole, sinking into a life where bragging about my child was my only joy. My parents lived that life. I didn't want it for myself. I should have realized that before I got the bright idea to get pregnant.

I was supposed to be modeling on the runways in Paris, making the top designers' clothes look stunning until I soaked up enough of their knowledge to create a line that soared above all of theirs. Instead, I was sitting in a medical office, getting complimented by nurses on how quickly my body snapped back after being stretched by the baby. They made sure to add that I looked fantastic throughout my whole pregnancy and should consider having another baby. I was never giving birth again, though. That was the longest 24 minutes of my life.

Banger's family said that they were going to help me with what I wanted to do, but those people couldn't stand me. If NyQuest wasn't Banger's baby, they had no reason to hold their promises to me, no matter how much money it got them. Leaning on the promises people made me in business settings was how I wound up thinking trapping someone with a baby was a good idea. I couldn't depend on anyone but me to make my dreams come true.

Surrendering to the thought that I was alone in the world almost made me cry. Banger stopped whatever he was saying to the doctor and pointed to my face.

"She looks like that most of the day, Doc. Look how beautiful she is. She don't need to look like that. What can I do?" Banger asked.

"Just let her rest for now. She's probably tired, and more than likely she's silently battling postpartum depression. It's rough, especially on someone with no history of depression," the doctor replied. "Is your job asking you to come back yet, Monaysia?"

I shrugged. "I have four more weeks of maternity leave with pay. Then, I can go unpaid for 12."

Before the doctor could say anything, Banger took a piece of paper from NyQuest's diaper bag to write down the instructions the doctor was going to give.

"Start with a lot of rest, and a lot of sunlight. I know that isn't always possible in our climate, but just let her go outside and walk for 20 minutes a day, at least. Let her take at least one walk by herself. She needs to get back to feeling like herself and can't do that if she's the only one with the baby," the doctor began.

Banger smiled, knowing he'd been doing the right thing all along.

"You ready to roll with your daddy even more, Quest?" he asked the newborn as though he'd answer him. "Mommy gotta get some rest to get her mind right, so you gotta come with me every morning."

I sighed, thinking about all the alone time that could possibly be in my future once those paternity test results came.

On our way home, we stopped by Banger's family's restaurant called Peter's Kitchen to get a meal. We sat by the portion of the Aliners River that was close to our apartment and ate with the windows rolled down. Then, he took NyQuest's stroller from the trunk, and we walked along the riverbank. That time, my silence was out of slight fear of that water. That river still creeped me out the way it sparkled and then bubbled in some places. The only other people who ever admitted to seeing the bubbling were Squeak and Rize. I found that if I agreed with Squeak about something, then it probably meant that I was going crazy.

Banger pushed the stroller, telling NyQuest about everything there was to see. He tried to include me in the conversation, but I didn't feel like talking. The police pulled beside us and asked us what we were doing there in the middle of the day, so we left.

The mailman was just leaving the lobby when we got home. I stopped to search through it. Among the bills were two letters from the Office of Vital Statistics. I clutched the envelopes while we rode the elevator. Banger looked down at my hands.

"I'm sending you to get your nails done. I'm tired of them shits not being airbrushed. Shouldn't you be doing cute-corny shit like getting our names and Quest's name on them?"

I looked down at my hands and realized how badly my nails were in need of a fill.

My hands were turning a faint shade of red from how tightly I was clutching them. He raised his eyebrows at that.

"Must be a check. You're holding onto those envelopes like they're money."

I forced a chuckle while I stepped off the elevator. I didn't even wait for him to put NyQuest in his swing or put the stroller away before I ripped the envelope open. My fingers trembled. Perspiration drizzled from my hairline. At first, I worried that it would smear my makeup. Then, I remembered that I was in such a funk that I forgot to put makeup on before I left the house. My breath caught in my throat, and I struggled to get the letter out of the envelope. When I read the results, they knocked me onto the couch. Immediately, I flipped over and sobbed while I held up the results for Banger to see.

"NyQuest is your son," I managed to say, and then started panting.

When my theatrics started to come down, I looked up at him. He still hadn't touched the paper to confirm anything. His face was stuck somewhere between surprised and puzzled.

"I know that. Now go take a nap. I'm tired of your face looking like you're about to cry all the damn time."

$1 from the sale of each copy of Here I Lay will be donated to Rise Above Poverty. Please consider making your own additional donation: https://www.riseabovepovertysyr.org/donate

Pushing my book babies into the world has not gotten any less surreal. That being said, there are countless people who made this possible. I won't be before you long.

First of all, I give all honor to God for giving me the talent of writing and putting this story in me. My prayer is that the people who need to read it find it in your time. I also pray that your time isn't the same time Zora started getting her flowers. The rent is due. Please let these books provide.

My husband Richard, you are the love of my life. The past 10 years have been amazing, and I'm looking forward to 10 million more.

To my children: Jemaine, Shateek, Riccardo, Raymoan, Rahmeelo, and Richara, being called Mommy is the highest honor.

To my mommy, Denise Smith: Thank you for becoming my biggest cheerleader.

To my father, Artis Smith, who passed away just two weeks before the completion of this work: I pray that your slumber is peaceful and that you are comfortable, free of tubes. I will remember you for who you were to me rather than your rewritten story.

To my family: There are too many of you to name without forgetting anyone, but I thank you all for being so supportive.

To the Girls' Night Out crew: You are the most amazing, best looking women in the world. I adore you!

Some really incredible people brought this book to life: Natasha Guy, my editor, your resilience is amazing. Nicole Watts of Kreations K, I am in awe of your brilliance and your patience. Kay Dupree, you are the best beta reader in the world.

There are authors who network, and then there are people who become your tribe. T. Styles & Cherisse, y'all are such an incredible vibe and excellent teachers. Portia Moore, thank you for giving me some direction. The Writers Who Write group — E, TK, Takara, and Markeshia — you are my family. I am eternally grateful for you beautiful ladies. Jana Jones, thank you for being someone I have something in common with in this world of writing and for sharing your platform with me. True to Urban Lit — especially Robin, Queen T, Lena B, D'Artanya Tisdale, Red Phenix, the Nicoles, and JoJo — thank you for showing me tremendous support. K. Sherrie, thank you for being so dope! Nicole Falls, Brenda Thomas, Kryss Clover, Cheryl Ferguson, LaShaunda Hoffman, Shonda Mayes, Allison Grace, Radiah Hubert, Kay, Shannon Humphrey, Merri Mayweather, Sable, Yvonne, Annette, Melissa, and Kiarra, you have the most beautiful souls imaginable. Jincey Lumpkins, I am so thankful that we crossed paths. Thank you to The Indie Authors' Conference for being there for me to ask questions every morning and share laughs every Friday.

Where would I be without my readers? If you have ever picked up one of my books or visited my website, I am grateful for you. I especially want to thank Diverse Shelves and Richard Ashby for taking chances on me. Melinda, you will never stop being my favorite.

Usually I thank every artist I listened to while writing my books, but there was one in particular who inspired this series from the titles to Monaysia Giles' quirky obsession:

Monica Denise Arnold, thank you for blessing the world with your voice!!!!

While I'm sure my head is forgetting somebody, my heart never will. I love and appreciate any and everybody who had anything to do with the creation of this book.

Kimani Lauren is an author determined to show how classism mirrors racism and then do something to destroy both. When she's not fixing the world, she enjoys being a wife, mother of 6, and searching for new methods to quiet her mind before she writes the next book. She loves tacos, mild buffalo wings (drums over flats), 90s music, and falling down internet rabbit holes. In a past life, she was a fashion designer. In this one, she can't draw to save her life. This is her fourth book, and she doesn't plan to stop any time soon.

If you love my work, please consider joining my email list. Subscribers receive the novellas in the series as a free gift of my appreciation a month prior to their release date as well as other exclusive content:

Website: https://www.kimanilaurenbooks.com[1]

Facebook: https://www.facebook.com/kimanilaurenbooks

Instagram: https://www.instagram.com/kimanilaurenbooks

Twitter: https://www.twitter.com/Kimanilaurenppw

Pinterest: https://www.pinterest.com/kimanilaurenbooks

1. https://www.kimanilaurenbooks.com/

For the first few months after NyQuest's birth, we were really happy. Watching the baby grow was the most interesting thing I'd done in my adult life. Every day, something different about him developed. When he finally opened his eyes and got some color, I started to see half of me and half of his daddy.

That is, when I got to see him. Most days, Banger got up in the morning and left, taking NyQuest with him. I wouldn't see them for hours. He said he was just trying to give me some time to sleep or some time to myself.

Most of the time, he came home with gifts for me. I still didn't have an armful of tennis bracelets like Selena, but one time he came home with a three-tiered nameplate with all of our names on it in huge cursive letters on a braided chain. He loved the Knicks, so I bought him a Patrick Ewing Jersey and made matching Knicks jackets for him and NyQuest. Making them matching clothes was my favorite thing to do, because he would put them on without hesitation.

He still sent me to get my hair and nails done weekly. Chillz's sisters were a lot nicer to me when I brought NyQuest in with me. Even Lynn halfway smiled at me when I sat in her chair and talked about being a mother.

Melinda and Selena always came into the shop when I was there. Selena started joining Melinda and me for our lunch dates. Neither of them ever let me pay for anything. Not only was I spoiled, I also had an extended family. They were okay once they stopped judging the hell out of me.

On Saturdays, we went to fish fries at Big Grams's house. Those fish fries were sometimes better than going to the club. After eating, the living room turned into a dance floor. Shondell was the DJ. Banger still didn't like to dance, but he swayed a little more with me. I kept my complaints about him not being more enthusiastic to myself.

I went to G-Ma's house to learn how to cook some of Banger's favorite meals, but that was too much work. I didn't want to spend my spare time in the kitchen. I had outfits to design and sew before my maternity leave ended. Peaches was getting better at sewing and making patterns, and we started taking custom orders for proms. I couldn't remember a time when I'd been happier in Sanford County.

And then Best paged me.

I don't know what made him remember that number after all of those months. Our last conversation left me thinking that we were done knowing each other at all.

My pager sat on the coffee table while Banger and I sat on the couch in the middle of a heated drawing competition. His picture of NyQuest put mine to shame, but we both had smiles on our faces as we drew. I expected it to be Kidra when my pager vibrated across the table and didn't pay attention, but it vibrated four more times.

"You ain't gonna hit that number back? Sounds important," Banger said.

I shook my head. “I don’t want no problems, and that sounds like a problem. A drunk one.”

Banger nodded his head and went back to drawing.

The number continued going off, so when Banger got a call for work that night, I waited about 20 minutes and then returned the call.

“Long time no talk,” Best slurred into the phone.

“What do you want, Best? I thought we were done dealing with each other. Go live your life. You’re about to get me in trouble, and I’m happy as hell with my boyfriend,” I said, and hung up the phone.

My mistake was forgetting to hit *67 before I dialed his number, so he had mine clear as day in his phone. He called back several times until I hissed for him not to call me anymore.

“Nay-Nay, please stop ignoring me! I miss you! Come smoke with me and let me eat you! I miss how you taste!”

I hung up the phone again, but he just called back. The phone ringing so much woke NyQuest. I cussed when I heard him on the baby monitor and went down the hall to get him.

“I just asked you to stop calling me, so please stop. I’m a mother and a wifey now,” I said.

Best laughed obnoxiously. “A wifey? That nigga know I was poking his baby in the head a couple of months ago?”

While I lifted NyQuest from his crib, Banger’s voice came over the phone, “I know now. I’m settin it on your ass when I see you.”

# Don't miss out!

Visit the website below and you can sign up to receive emails whenever Kimani Lauren publishes a new book. There's no charge and no obligation.

https://books2read.com/r/B-A-JPBO-WKJPB

BOOKS 2 READ

Connecting independent readers to independent writers.

# Also by Kimani Lauren

**Secrets From the Bridge**

Red Danger Days

Here I Lay Part 1: I've Gotta Have It

## About the Publisher

Perfectly Polished Words, established 2010. Because perfection is *almost* good enough.

www.ingramcontent.com/pod-product-compliance
Lightning Source LLC
LaVergne TN
LVHW091144080826
845145LV00008B/2250

* 9 7 8 1 7 3 6 9 5 3 9 3 8 *